G000075372

Breeze

by Sarah Asuquo

London | New York

Published by Clink Street Publishing 2020

First edition.

ISBN:
978-1-913568-40-5 - paperback
978-1-913568-41-2 - ebook

Dedicated to every young person I've been privileged to work with throughout my career. You inspire me daily. This one's for you.

Miss A.

−1−

Track Girl

Breeze's self-labelled 'trend-indifference' is a trait that she has lived with, and was somewhat grateful for, since she was a child. The term refers to the recurring social situations Breeze would often find herself in that caused her to question whether her peers were... um, what's the right word? Weirdos. Yes, weirdos. Or if she was in fact the oddball who failed to see the world in the same way that everyone else did. At times, Breeze thought that it might be a Tower Hamlets thing and that everyone in her borough was just a bit, what do you call it? Loopy. She once hypothesised that perhaps the prolonged inhalation of the oil emitted into the air by the local chippys' deep fat fryers, combined with the aromas of the rapidly decaying meat thoughtfully hung out on display in the local markets, infused with the remnant scents of the intermittent sewer leaks in the area had a greater effect on the local residents than they had realised. A real conundrum. Well, for Breeze it was.

Ultimately, Breeze had always been different, and she was ok with that. Take preschool, for example. Whilst most children were mesmerised by Ziggy, the magic puppet, Breeze was entertained by talking to insects. This wasn't an issue — until she decided to invite the insects to Story Time, sending every child in the book corner into a screaming, crying frenzy! Every child that is except Gerry Ginger. Gerry just ate the insects, which made Breeze cry.

Primary school was no different. Breeze had an imaginary friend named AJ. Pretty normal, right? Everyone had an imaginary friend who they shared all their secrets with, played tag with and gave half of their packed lunch to… no? Turns out that their friendship wasn't so common after all and soon, AJ became Breeze's only friend.

Breeze now attended Aspire Academy, a federation of five secondary schools in East London, and she was a student of the school in Poplar. Although secondary school had been a better experience for Breeze, she still didn't feel like she belonged; she wasn't like most of the girls in her school. The most popular girls were the 'slayed girls', who firmly believed that wearing makeup in public was mandatory and had the essential, daily duty of ensuring that their bestie's "contour was poppin'." But the thought of applying anything other than cocoa butter to her skin unsettled Breeze's soul. Then there were the 'academic girls', who would adamantly search for any reason to start a debate and whose sole aim in life was to prove that they were the most intelligent beings in the room. The 'rebels', who went above and beyond to highlight how different they were to the rest of the students at Aspire, which Breeze thought slightly defeated the point because they were identically unique, if that makes sense. The 'science girls', who spent their free time precariously experimenting, with the hope to make the next, ground-breaking scientific discovery. The 'performing arts girls', also known as the 'creatives', who made a song and dance out of everything, literally. The 'IT girls', who could effortlessly hack into every software system within the school, a skill they often used to cause havoc (just google "Aspire Academy Host Hip-hop Festival during GCSE Examinations"). The 'selective mutes', who didn't speak to anyone other than the members of their friendship group. The 'bad girls' who, based on the self-proclaimed name, Breeze assumed were bad in some way. And that was just the girls. The boys had even more squads! Breeze just couldn't find a group that she could fit into and she was fine with that. Every week, there was a new song that supposedly 'banged' or dance craze or social media challenge, and Breeze couldn't keep up! To be honest, she didn't want to. She would rather spend her spare time dancing and rapping along to MC Hammer classics with her family than listening to the ramblings of the illustrious rapper, Yung Coin, also known as YC. Yes, you read that correctly. There is no 'o' in young. And no, his music was not acceptable.

As she sat in her maths lesson daydreaming, Breeze was blissfully unaware that her class were playing 'whippin', a game in which one person discreetly performs any gesture related to driving without being detected by the teacher and then passes it on someone else. Sounds fun, right? Not for Breeze. She neither enjoyed nor understood the game.

"Why is this even a thing?" she would furtively protest. "None of us can drive! ... But we're not even in cars, though. We're in chairs — very uncomfortable chairs!" were just a few of the thoughts that rang through her mind when she watched the game.

Jayden looked over his shoulder as he pretended to reverse parallel park his car (his car being his desk, obviously) whilst everyone in the class watched in admiration. Everyone except Breeze. Breeze wasn't watching and consequently, she missed Jayden wink at her (that's how you pass it on... I know). After a few exaggerated winks, Breeze heard a voice in the distance cry "Track Girl... Track Girl" except, it wasn't in the distance; it was Chanel, the most popular girl in Breeze's year group. Breeze snapped out of her daydream, which she wasn't happy about because she had finally persuaded MC Hammer to teach her the 'Hammer Dance' and she had almost mastered it.

"It's your go," said Chanel as Breeze looked at her in bewilderment. "Whippin'," she continued, accompanied with what Breeze called the 'angry mum neck roll' because this game was clearly the most sensible and appropriate activity that students should be doing in a maths lesson.

All eyes were on Breeze. She looked to Mr Fraser to save her from the madness, but to her dismay, he wasn't looking back. "Don't do it to yourself, Breeze. It's such a stupid game, don't succumb to the pressure" she thought to herself, but her hands did not comply and before she knew it, Breeze was pressing an imaginary car horn (yep, I know) and if that wasn't enough, for some reason, Breeze thought it would be a good idea to add sound effects to what had always been a *silent* game by uncomfortably sounding through a forced smile, "beep, beep." It wasn't.

"Not beep!" said Mr Fraser in his Jamaican-Cockney accent. "I said *keep*, keep your exercise books and I'll collect them next lesson."

The class found this hysterical, and a storm of laughter swept through the classroom as Mr Fraser ended the lesson.

"Ah, you're so funny, Track Girl," said Chanel, leaving the room, her flock sniggering behind her.

"No. I'm not funny," Breeze murmured. "James Corden: funny, Kojo Anim: funny." Breeze knew that she wasn't funny, and that was ok.

Breeze also knew that she was a 'Track Girl' and being called one wasn't a problem. However, as much as Breeze loved being on the track and it was one of the few places where she felt like she actually belonged, she knew that Chanel didn't call her Track Girl because she admired her athletic ability, but rather because she could not remember Breeze's name, and that was not ok.

-2-

VIPs Only

The discovery of Breeze's ability to sprint occurred in unconventional circumstances. It was her first day of secondary school and her older cousin, Zach, who lived in the estate opposite to hers, picked her up to walk her there. As they came out of the entrance to her block, Breeze warned Zach about Kasper, the ferocious terrier of Lockley Estate, from number 305. The slightest noise would send him barking mad, literally, rampantly chasing the culprit of disturbance of the peace. Ironic as the noise he made would always be the cause of a commotion.

"Wait!" Breeze whispered.

"Come on, man!" Zach insisted. "I ain't scared of no dog. As long as you're rolling with me, you're all good. You don't need to worry 'bout — woah, what the hell is that, Bree? — "

An incidental step on a twig triggered a viscous growl that echoed through the compound, accompanied by the sound of Kasper's paws accelerating on the ground as he charged towards them. By the time Breeze had recovered from her state of shock and looked to her left, Zach had disappeared.

"Run, Breeze! Run!" yelled Zach.

But her feet would not move.

"Breeze! Run, baby!" her mother cried from her bedroom window. "Hey! Hey! Control your dog!"

Breeze was paralysed with fear, her senses obscured as her mother's screams were interchanged with Kasper's barking, which was overridden by the pulse of her heart and the blood-curdling sight of Kasper's canines, displayed to her in fury.

"Ahh!" she screamed, and her body reacted in flight mode. Within seconds she had caught up with Zach, narrowly escaping a perilous fate.

"Breezy! How did you run so quickly?"

"How-could-you-just-leave-me-like-that?"

"Sorry, cuz. It was just my natural reaction. But that was crazy, though. You were mad quick! Are you ok?"

"Yeah. Yeah, I'm cool."

This day gave Breeze a newfound sense of confidence. For the first time in her life, she had rescued herself from danger. She started to compete in her school's sporting events and very quickly, her P.E. teachers recognised her talent. Boy, could she run! Breeze had found her gift, her 'thing' and soon, the track became her most treasured companion.

***

Breeze and Bella, or B Squared (as they, and only they, liked to call themselves) just understood one another. They met in Year 7 when they bumped into each other at the school's mini pond. This was the perfect location for them to eat their lunch as they both found the canteen too boisterous to endure and were pleasantly surprised when they discovered someone else who also knew that the place existed. No one went to the school's pond. It was located behind the library, which was also desolate at lunchtimes, and soon it became B Squared's spot. Their friendship was sealed by their equal and unwavering love for Ben & Jerry's ice cream (cookie dough flavour, of course) and their aversion to cruisin' (the older version of whippin'… don't ask). They even shared the same birthday, 02.02.2002, because, as they would say, "the best things come in twos".

"Easy Breezy! Let's go! The arena awaits!" said Bella.

Bella had energy for days; it didn't take much to get her excited and at times, Breeze would have to use strategies she had learned from watching *Toddlers, Tears & Tantrums* to calm her down. However, on this occasion, Bella's excitement was justified as this was another passion that B Squared shared, athletics. They both competed in the National Junior League. Bella had the leading score for javelin in the Borough, and Breeze was 1st nationally for the 100-metre sprint. Fortunately, Aspire Academy was a sports specialist institution, with a state-of-the-art training ground and B Squared trained there after school on Tuesdays and Thursdays. As they made their way to the arena, Breeze explained the 'beep, beep' incident.

"Don't lie, Breezy!" Bella winced in disappointment, placing her head in her hands. "You actually said 'beep, beep'. Why? Just why? Better from you, Breezy. Better — from — you."

"I know, Bell. I know. Don't make me feel worse."

"All right. All right. But seriously, though, I just don't get the game," said Bella.

"That's what I'm saying!"

"None of us can drive!" they clamoured simultaneously.

"Girls, you only have an hour; I need to lock up early today," said the school's caretaker. He admired B Squared's commitment to training and would often close the stadium slightly later so that they could train for longer.

"Ok, Bossman. Thanks!" said Breeze.

"We'll be done by then, Boss," Bella replied.

"He's so safe, man. What's his name again?"

"I can't remember, you know. I swear it's on his cap."

"Is it?"

"Yeah, I'm sure I've seen it before."

"Oh, ok. I'll make sure to check it out next time."

"Yeah, but come on, let's get started. We don't have much time."

"Cool. Let's go."

Bella watched in amazement as Breeze shot past her in pursuit of the finish line, her braids soaring behind her, as swift as an unexpected gale. "No way," she whispered.

"She's a beast!" said Jayden, heading towards the sandpit. He was every girl's crush at Aspire Academy. Well, almost every girl. B Squared were not interested. They could appreciate that he was 'easy on the eyes', as Breeze would say, and watching him compete in the long jump was impressive, but his overconfidence was off-putting and consequently, any interaction between B Squared and Jayden was limited to small talk. "In a bit, Belly," he said, accompanied with an awkward high five.

"It's Bella… he knows it's Bella. Bell, Bells even B would be acceptable, but Belly! Really?" Bella muttered.

"How did I do, Bell?" asked Breeze, panting and kneeling in exhaustion.

Bella snapped out of her rant and looked down at her stopwatch. Her face was deliberately void of expression (for dramatic effect, of course) as she jogged towards her bestie.

"It's not about the time you achieved, Breezy... as long as you tried your best... that's all that matters, right? That's what's most important... FIFTEEN POINT TWO NINE SECONDS! C'MON!" she yelled, jolting Breeze's shoulders.

"What! That's a new PB!" Breeze jumped up and did her celebratory dance (MC Hammer's 'Shuffle Dance') followed by the B Squared handshake (smooth arm slide, twinkle fingers, hand clench, fist pump, and explosion – this sequence and having accurate timing was imperative).

"Aww, that's *really* cool," chuckled a voice in the distance with sarcasm oozing from every syllable within each word.

"Chanel," said B Squared in unison, slowly turning their heads towards her direction, hoping that they were wrong. They weren't.

"Hey girlies, you look... interesting," (really? Of all the adjectives). "The weather's nice, isn't it?" she asked, scanning the arena like a wanted criminal.

It was clear she was up to something and Breeze couldn't bear the pretences any longer. "So, what's up, Chanel? Have you come to train with us?" A silly question and Breeze knew it was. Especially as Chanel was wearing her school pumps and holding her designer handbag like a mother cradling a new-born.

Chanel fake laughed excessively. "No silly, I'm here to give you guys this invitation." Breeze and Bella looked at each other in disbelief; they were never invited to anything. "Well... aren't you going to ask what it's for?" said Chanel, full of elation.

Unimpressed that she was being treated like a five-year-old, Bella replied in a monotone voice, "What's it for, Chanel?"

"My birthday party! The third of the third because *three* is a magic number!"

Bella and Breeze looked at each other with the mutual understanding that there were no such thing as magic numbers, but if there were, two would be a clear choice.

"Thanks, Chanel. That's nice of you to invite us," replied Bella, still in shock.

Chanel guffawed even louder than before. B Squared were confused but thought that pretending to laugh along with her would make the situation less uncomfortable. It didn't.

"Why are we laughing?" said Breeze through clenched teeth.

"I don't know," muttered Bella through her forced smile.

"The invite isn't for you two, it's for Jayden!" said Chanel. "My birthday party, as in *my* sweet 15th birthday! It will be the biggest and littest event of the year! VIPs only."

"So why are you giving us an invitation for Jayden?" asked Breeze, dryly.

"Because he's my crush, duh!" Breeze and Bella looked at Chanel blankly. "Look, I can't give him the invitation myself, that's too keen. You've got to keep them on their toes, you know?" she said, as if this was a rational explanation. "So, I need *you* two to give it to him… please? You train with him anyway so it should be easy, right?"

"Nah, we don't, actually. Not re-"

"Thank you so much, girls! Aww, that's so cute that you actually thought you were invited… bless," she said as she hugged them and gave them an air double French kiss (another thing B Squared disliked and didn't understand).

"No. Not cute. Puppies: cute, babies: cute, Year 7s on their first day of secondary school and their extra-large rucksacks: cute," Breeze mumbled to herself as she watched Chanel perform her strut of satisfaction. B squared knew that they were not cute, and that was ok.

"VIPs only, you know. So cheeky!" said Bella.

"Yeah, typical Chanel. But you know what, it don't matter," replied Breeze, "We've got our own birthdays coming up in a few weeks anyway. Who needs Chanel's sweet 15th? Ain't no sweeter than Ben & Jerry's Cookie Dough Ice Cream!"

"You're right. Let's just give this invitation to Jayden and forget about it. I say on the third of the third, when most people will be at Chanel's party, we do our own thing. Pizza, ice cream, a movie and *my* VIP," said Bella.

"Who's that, then?" said Breeze, grinning subtly. "Aww, you're such a softy!" Bella was unimpressed by her bestie's mockery. "I'm only playing with you, Bell. That sounds like a plan. You're the only VIP I need!" Breeze's expression of mischief progressively transitioned to a look of deep thought. "Bell... do me a favour."

"What?" asked Bella.

"When you like a guy, or whoever..."

"Yeah..."

"Please be normal."

"I will, Breezy. I will. Promise."

"Me too."

Their mutual understanding of what was meant by 'normal' was crystal clear and they index swore to seal their agreement (because pinky swearing was outdated and childish).

−3−

02.02.2017

The first birthday Breeze could remember was when she turned three. Most of the day was a blur, but she remembered wearing a bright green and black, polka dot dress with frills and shoulder pads embodying a fusion of the 80s. She was in her living room, standing on a small stall, surrounded by her cousins, aunts, and uncles as they sang 'Happy Birthday' to her. Her mother knelt in front of her holding a cake whilst her father cradled her younger brother, JJ who was terrified by the candlelight. "Happy birthday, dear Breezy, happy birthday to you."

"Go on, baby. Blow... blow... and make a wish," her mother prompted.

Breeze was too young to understand the idea of making a wish, but she did understand that it was her special day and that her whole family were there just for her. She filled her cheeks with as much air as possible and blew ardently as they all clapped. Breeze remembered how loved she felt on that day.

As Breeze grew older, she became increasingly aware of the financial difficulties her parents had. She would attend the flamboyant birthday parties of her friends and family. The bouncy castles, face painting, clowns, excessive amounts of food, not to mention the endless presents, were juxtaposed to the birthdays in the Bassey household. When they hosted parties at her home, Breeze would overhear the comments made by the adult guests to her parents.

"This is intimate, innit?"

"Yeah, nice and cosy," her mother would reply, masking her annoyance.

"You should have said things were tight, bro. I would've lent you some cash."

"We're all good, thanks," said her father, "I don't need no handouts. I can look after me and mine."

Eventually, the invites to their extended family and friends diminished. However, every year, without fail, her parents made sure that they celebrated Breeze's and JJ's birthdays as a family. It was important to their parents that they always had a birthday cake, blew out their candles and made a wish. Breeze's favourite cakes were the ones her mother made herself. She remembered how upset her mother was one year because she had spent hours looking for the perfect recipe and baking a cake for her, but briefly fell asleep whilst it was in the oven and it overcooked. Breeze didn't mind though, in fact, she loved the extra crunch.

"It's like a cookie, crumble cake, Mum! I love it."

"Are you sure, baby? I can run to the shop and buy another one."

"No Mum, it's perfect!"

And with a little buttercream icing, the cake was a hit for the whole family too. Her parents also made sure that Breeze and her brother opened a gift on their birthdays, no matter how small it was. At times, although she didn't express it, this was upsetting for Breeze. She saw how hard her parents worked and thought it was unfair that her family had less than others. Breeze didn't ask for much and so she didn't understand why her parents couldn't just buy her the only present that she wanted on her one special day of the year. But with maturity, she began to appreciate the effort that her parents made, the time that they spent together as a family, the love that filled their home. And soon, she realised that this was the greatest gift of all.

***

"Happy birthday, dear Breezy, happy birthday to you. Make a wish, baby."

"Thank you, Mama!" said Breeze, searching her bedroom for her gift.

"Make a wish first, baby," her mother chuckled. "This year we're going to choose your gift together," she explained.

For the last two months, Breeze had requested one thing for her birthday: the new Jordan Air Swift trainers in burgundy. So, when she awoke to see mother holding a cake instead of a gift-wrapped shoebox, she couldn't help but feel slightly deflated. Nevertheless, it was a delicious Victoria sponge cake with buttercream icing and the day wasn't over yet so, in one smooth breath, Breeze blew out her candles, made a wish and bear hugged her mother.

"Happy birthday, big head," said Breeze's little brother. Little may be an unsuited adjective because JJ was much taller than Breeze and there was only one year, eleven months and two days between them, a fact Breeze often pointed out. "Got you a lil' something, something," he said, handing her a Tesco's bag.

"Woi! Skittles, Tangtastic Haribo's, Thai sweet chilli Sensations, Maltesers, pineapple KA and Ben & Jerry's cookie dough ice cream! Ah man, I'm gonna get emosh. You got all my favourites. Thanks, bro!" she said, bear hugging JJ this time.

"It's cool, sis," he replied, gently trying to escape her grip.

"Your dad is on the phone, darling," said Breeze's mother.

"Thank God for that," JJ exhaled.

"Happy birthday, my baby!" her father exclaimed.

"Thank you, Pops!"

"Now I know you had something very particular in mind for your gift, but Mum and I think you'll like what we have chosen instead. However, if your mind is set on the Jordans, you can get them. All I ask is that you're open to at least consider what we have selected."

Breeze couldn't tell if her parents were being serious or doing that thing where they pretend that they haven't gotten her what she wanted and then shout, "ta-da!" whilst revealing her original request. Despite her confusion, she decided to play along.

"Ok Pops, I'll be open minded," she replied.

"That's all we ask. Have a good day and I'll see you this evening."

"Later, Pops."

"Go B squared, go B squared, go! Second of Feb's our day, yo!" cheered Breeze and Bella through their phones.

"No mushy stuff, but you're the bestest!" said Bella.

"You're even Bella!" said Breeze. The car became silent. "That was bad wasn't it?"

"Yes," said Bella and Breeze's mother.

"But just for today, I'll allow you," said Bella.

"Thanks for being so forgiving, Bell," replied Breeze in her jestingly serious voice. "I deeply appreciate your understanding in this matter. Anyway, I'm in the car with Mum so I'll see you later, ok."

"Ok. Later, Breezy."

"Really? *Even Bella*," continued Breeze's mother.

"I know, Mum… I know."

They began to slow down and as her mother parked the car, Breeze searched the area, attempting to work out where they were.

"Almost there!" said Breeze's mother as they walked down what was beginning to feel like the longest street in Hackney. Although Breeze wasn't one to shy away from physical activity, this walk had become insufferable and just as Breeze was about to ask if they were there yet, for the third time, her mother exclaimed, "We're here!"

They were standing outside AK (Alternative Kicks), a sports store in Dalston. AK was not the most popular choice for teenagers and Breeze found it difficult to hide her bemusement.

"Breeze, your father and I have always admired your confidence to be yourself rather than blindly following the latest trend," explained Breeze's mother. "Jordan's are really cool right now, everyone's wearing them and if that's what you want, you can have them too. But your dad and I just wanted you to have a look at what else was out there so that you can at least consider all of your options and be sure that those are the trainers you want."

Breeze knew that she wanted her Js, but she understood her parents' point and agreed to look around the store. Besides, there were no trainers that would even compare to the ones she wanted, right?

After 20 minutes in AK, Breeze had made up her mind. "These shoes are cool, Mum, but they ain't the Jordan's Air Swifts."

"Fair enough, Breeze, let's go to Foot Locker and get them for you."

However, just as they were leaving, Breeze noticed something glowing in the corner of the store. "What's that?" she asked.

"What?" said her mother.

"Over there, can't you see it? They're glowing."

"I can't see it, my dear, must be my age!"

But it wasn't her mother's age. What Breeze didn't know was that she was the only one in the store who could see that the trainers were glowing. As she picked them up for further inspection, Breeze was amazed. "These are cold!" she said, delicately turning them around.

"Cold is a good thing, right?" whispered her mother to the Sale's Assistant, who gave her a gentle nod and a wink of confirmation.

"Look, Mum, there's a 'B' on one shoe and a '2' on the other," said Breeze as she wore them. "Rah! They fit perfectly and I love the burgundy! ... I want these, Mum — I mean, can I have these ones, please?"

"Are you sure? What about your Jordans?"

"Nah, I want these instead, Mum. They're perfect, proper comfortable and the grip is certi!" Her mother looked over to the Sale's Assistant who confirmed that certi was also a good thing with a discreet thumbs up. "These will be sick for running!" And just like that, the Jordan Air Swifts were a desire of the past. "Thank you, Mum! Thanks for helping make the best decision for me."

"You're welcome, baby. We knew you would."

Later that evening, Breeze and her family made their way to Bella's family home. Each year, on their birthdays, they would take it in turns to go to each other's houses and celebrate their special day together. It was tradition, and this year it was Bella's turn to host. The evening consisted of dinner, cake, chocolate, and ice cream. Alongside charades, karaoke, dancing and *The Adventures of Star Girl*, B Squared's favourite movie series. The events of the night must have taken its toll on everyone as they were all asleep in the living room. Everyone except Breeze and Bella. They crept upstairs to Bella's bedroom and jumped on her bed.

"We're fifteen, Bell! That's crazy," said Breeze.

"I know, right? We've grown up so quickly," replied Bella, pretending to cry.

"Stop that! You sound like my mum," Breeze snapped, throwing a pillow at her. "Anyhoo, have you had a good day, Bell? What did your parents get you?"

"Yeah, man. Today's been the best birthday yet! I got the most beautiful earrings, look." Bella pulled her hair back behind her ears, revealing letter B studs with Swarovski Crystals.

"Wow, those are lovely."

"Thanks, Breeze. How about you? Did you get the Jordans?"

"No. I could have, but my parents wanted me to check out some other kicks first and I chose these bad boys instead," Breeze explained, clicking her heels like Dorothy.

"They're cold!"

"That's what I said!"

Breeze stood up and did the 'Shuffle Dance', demonstrating how skilfully she could move in her new trainers. Suddenly, she lost her balance and fell over. Bella chuckled as she helped her up, but Breeze instantly fell to the floor again.

"That's weird," said Bella. "They're glowing."

"You see it too?"

"Well it's hard to miss!"

"That's what I thought, but my family couldn't see it when I tried to show them earlier," said Breeze as she fought to take a step.

"You look like Bambi!" said Bella, holding in her laughter because she saw that Breeze was genuinely struggling to walk.

Abruptly, the trainers stopped glowing and Breeze regained her balance. The girls stared at each other, trying to understand what had just happened.

"Breeze, Bella, come down, please. It's getting late," called Breeze's father.

"Coming!" cried Breeze. "We need to speak about this... don't tell anyone."

"Promise," said Bella as they index swore and ran downstairs.

The Announcement

'Unforeseen circumstances… what does that even mean?' said Breeze.

As the Principal addressed the school, Breeze felt as though she was in a trance. Mrs Banjo's words were muffled as they arduously travelled through the continuous murmuring of the 'slayed girls' and the suffocating abundance of the Lynx Africa deodorant in the air from the basketball team.

"Whilst I appreciate your disappointment," explained Mrs Banjo, void of expression, "the situation is beyond my control. Without disclosing too much information and breaching the contractual terms, our founders have decided that they will no longer fund our sporting incentives and believe that our school should move towards developing a more… *traditional* based specialism. Therefore, we will no longer be a sporting specialist academy and our arena will be closed at the end of this academic year. We will, however, go ahead with our upcoming Regional Athletic Heats and annual Federation Sports' Day, which, as per tradition, will involve all Aspire Academies in East London and will be held here, in our training grounds for the last time. Let's make these final events as successful and memorable as possible."

The assembly hall erupted in a succession of astonishment, fury, and gloom.

"Nah, you can't be serious! What do you mean, Miss?" questioned Jayden.

"That's really sad… No more bicep appreciation days, boy," said Chanel as her friends shook their heads in disapproval. "What? It's true."

"Furthermore, I will be stepping down as your Principal this summer and would now like to introduce my replacement, Dr Maximus," Mrs Banjo explained, struggling to contain her emotions. She scurried off the stage and Dr Maximus approached the pulpit.

"Why is my man wearing a robe, though? He's doing the most right now," said Ade.

"Good afternoon, all. Usually, I expect my students to stand when I enter a room and be seated upon my request. However, I will train you all accordingly upon my official arrival in September. I look forward to working with you all."

"Train? Are we dogs?" Armani snarled.

"Maximus... he must mean *Maximum*! Why's he being so extra?" Ade grumbled.

"I can't believe Mrs B is just giving up on us like this. That didn't even sound like her, she sounded like she's been brainwashed," said Bella. Breeze did not respond; she was overcome with heartache. "Breezy? ... Breeze?"

"I just can't right now, Bell... I can't."

Bella held Breeze's hand, comforting them both. A solemn stillness suffused the assembly hall. Although sport was not a talent that every student possessed, it unified Aspire Academy. Everyone looked forward to the school's sporting events. Whether a competitor, a performer or a spectator, sport brought the school together. There were no 'groups' or 'squads'; Aspire were a united team. As it dawned upon the students that this historical aspect of their schooling experience was soon coming to an end, the grief was communal. No words were required and for the first time, without instruction from the staff, the students of Aspire Academy remained silent.

– 5 –

Magic

Two weeks had passed since the news of the arena closure and although the morale of staff and students was low, there was a united agreement to honour the sporting history of Aspire Academy and make the final two events greater than ever before. The art group were on banner duty, the creatives were preparing dance routines and the music team were planning to get a steel pan band to perform. Even the canteen staff were involved and promised to provide a plethora of food including the students' favourites: patties, jerk chicken and jollof rice! B Squared vowed to do their part and trained relentlessly to prepare for the days. Breeze had been running in her new trainers and had mastered how to maintain her balance in them. As B Squared jogged around the stadium to warm up, Breeze's trainers began to illuminate.

"These kicks are so comfy, Bell. I feel like I'm running on clouds when I wear them."

"Oh yeah? Bet I'll still beat you to the finish line!" Bella jested as she brusquely ran into Breeze, causing her to stumble, and raced towards the finish line.

"This girl never learns!" Breeze chuckled, leaping to her feet in Bella's pursuit.

"Can't catch me, I'm the gingerbread girl!"

Breeze pelted towards Bella, and the distance between them rapidly decreased. As she overtook Bella and crossed the finish line, her speed intensified.

"All right, show-off. You're doing too much now. Chill," Bella groaned as Breeze began another lap around the arena. "Breeze... It's ok, you can stop now."

"No, I can't!" she cried.

Breeze's feet mirrored those of a Looney Tunes character; from a distance, her legs became a tornado.

"Stop, Breeze!" The concern grew increasingly apparent on Bella's face.

"I'm trying to! I can't! Help me!"

After two laps of the track, Breeze came to a sudden halt.

"What was that?" asked Bella.

"I have no idea! I ran after you and it felt normal and then... then... I don't know. It's like my feet just took over."

"You're not even out of breath. That's crazy."

"I know. It's like I was running, but *I* wasn't running... you get me?"

"Yeah, I get you. I think."

"That's mad. I — I. Nah, don't worry."

"Nah, say it, Breeze. You...?"

"It's just... these kicks. They... I'm starting to think that they're... like you know..." Breeze was hesitant to utter the word, "magical."

B Squared were dazed by the possibility that magic existed. Although they didn't speak, their trail of thought was identical. Once they processed what Breeze had said, they realised how absurd their thoughts were and roared with laughter.

"Ahh, man. You're a joker! Magic, you know. There's no such thing, Breezy!"

"I know. I know, but this just doesn't make sense, Bell."

"I hear that, Breeze. It's weird. They even glow and all sorts, but magic... could it be?"

They stared at each other, deeply considering if what they had always believed was impossible was actually feasible, and in unison they both whispered, "Nah".

–6–

Rumour Has It

The Regional Athletic Heats were a week away and Breeze had completely grasped how to use her trainers. She could now control her acceleration and when she triggered the customised pressure points within the soles, Breeze could run up to 100 miles per hour! Bella had tried on the trainers (B Squared had the same shoe size, another commonality), but they didn't activate for her feet; they didn't even glow when she wore them. The shoes were destined for Breeze, and they both knew that. Breeze had decided that she would never trigger the speed function in her trainers for athletic purposes because she wanted to be sure that she had an accurate judgement of her progress and sprint timings. The fit, cushioning, and anti-slip grip features (as well as the splash of burgundy) made Breeze's trainers ideal for running. Once they were on her feet, she felt complete and ready to take on the track.

"On your marks. Get set. Go!" Bella instructed. Breeze was a bolt of lightning, striking past Bella as she crossed the finish line.

"Fifteen point five seconds," said Bella, aware that Breeze would be disappointed. Although Breeze was the current national champion for the 100-metre sprint, there were endless rumours spreading through the school about a girl, called Tanya, from the Aspire Academy in Homerton, who had the potential to defeat Breeze this year. According to Chanel, who wasn't the most reliable source, Tanya's personal best was fifteen point five seconds, only two seconds longer than Breeze's and Breeze knew that she would have work hard to maintain her title.

"Don't stress about it, Breeze. We've trained so much recently. Maybe your body just needs a break."

"Yeah, I think you're right."

"I always am," she joked. "Anyway, I'm marvin', mate."

"Same."

"Let's go to Uncle D's, he promised us a free meal time ago!"

"Oh yeah. It's true, you know! Let's go... *After* you practice your javelin throw."

"But I'm so hungry!" Bella pleaded.

"So am I. So, hurry up!"

"Ah, man. Fine," Bella whimpered, dragging her feet.

"What? Did you think I was the only one training today? Behave, darlin'!"

The Regional Athletic Heats

"Come on, Bella!" Breeze cheered, with every particle of oxygen within her lungs.

Steadily, Bella jogged across the runway towards the marked boundary, her javelin a Peltast's spear. As she released her javelin towards the skies and regained her balance, it soared and then descended like an eagle's glide.

"Sixty-eight point two seven metres." The commentator's voice pierced through the tannoy megaphone, sparking the celebration of the crowd around the arena, but the sound that was most prominent to Bella was the roaring and prolonged "YES!" of her best friend.

"That's my bestie, you know!" Breeze boasted to random members of the crowd. "That's my best friend."

Bella pounced on Breeze and they fell to the ground. "I've beaten my PB, Breezy! I did it!"

"I knew you would, Bell. That's the best score in your event as well. I'm so proud of you!"

"Thanks, Breeze. Now c'mon, track events in five. Go and boss it!"

The B Squared handshake gave Breeze the boost that she needed. She tied up her braids as she walked towards the track and approached her opponents.

"You all right? My name's Tanya. I'm from Aspire in–"

"Homerton," Breeze interrupted.

"Yeah."

"Yeah, I'm all right. Welcome to our school."

"This arena is *so* sick! You lot are lucky to have it. I don't think any other Aspire Academy has facilities like this."

"Yeah, it's a shame they're closing it down."

"I heard about that. That's proper sad," said Tanya.

"Yeah. We're all gutted… So, I hear you're quite the runner."

"I've heard the same about you."

The girls' eyes alternated between each other and the stadium as they both thought of the next appropriate thing to say.

"Good luck," they both said.

"You too," they replied together, followed by a brief and subtle grin. In that moment, their nerves were shared, and their smiles signified their respect for each other.

Mr Peters approached the track, his megaphone in one hand, a starting pistol in the other. "On your marks. Get set. Go!"

The shot fired and they were off! Breeze and Tanya were significantly ahead of their competitors. Initially, Breeze was in the lead, but Tanya was rapidly closing in on her. The finish line felt like it was miles away. Breeze and Tanya were now adjacent to each other.

"Come on, Breezy. You've got this," whispered Bella, concerned about her best friend's fate.

Breeze's focus faltered and she found herself frequently looking over at Tanya beside her… then behind her… then beside her again… and then, in front of her. Breeze panicked. Suddenly, she blasted ahead and overtook Tanya. She crossed the finish line in first place and continued running around the stadium. The crowd cheered in astonishment. Chants of Breeze's name resounded through the arena and before she realised, Breeze was surrounded by Aspire students she didn't know existed.

"That was sick! How did you do that?" asked Ming.

"You just blasted out of nowhere for the second half of the race!" Jason exclaimed.

"I couldn't even see your creps anymore, Breeze. They were all blurry and ting!" Ade yelled.

"I rate that, B. You're a G," said Jayden.

Even Daisy, a member of the 'selective mutes' who sat next to Breeze in Science, approached Breeze and covertly said, "Good job."

"Thanks, Daisy. You all right?"

Daisy didn't respond and rushed back to the stands, but Breeze was touched and grateful for the words she had received.

"That was cool, Track Girl. Here," said Chanel, handing Breeze an envelope. "I think that race deserves V.I.P. status. *Now*, you can come to my party."

"Really! Thanks, Chanel. Can Bella come as well?"

"Is Bella a V.I.P.? Uh, No. She can't come," she snarled.

Tanya graciously approached Breeze and without speaking, shook her hand. The sadness she felt was palpable and suddenly, Breeze's victory didn't feel so great. As the crowd dispersed, Breeze could see Bella looking at her in disappointment. Timidly, Breeze walked towards her bestie and was met with two words that ran through her body and filled every part of her being with guilt:

"You cheated."

"No… I …"

Bella shook her head and left the stadium, leaving Breeze standing alone with her thoughts.

"I cheated."

–8–

Jealous

Breeze had always loved being a big sister; it was a responsibility that she took very seriously. She would help her parents look after JJ as much as she could. From fetching the changing bag, to singing to him as he fell asleep, Breeze was always ready to help. Anytime she heard him crying, she would race to the nearest parent and alert them by repeating, "Baby cry, baby cry, baby cry" until they responded. Eventually, Breeze learned how to comfort JJ on her own. She would do the 'chicken dance' and cluck away until he stopped. It worked every time. Their bond was special, but at times, Breeze found being a big sister challenging. Things began to change, and Breeze didn't understand why. For instance, when Breeze was three, she was given her own bedroom. Her mum yelled, "ta-da!" as she revealed the safari-themed decor, which excited Breeze initially, until she noticed one thing: a single bed.

"But Mummy, where will you and Daddy and JJ sleep?"

"We'll be right next door, my love."

"But I like putting JJ to sleep and sleeping in your room."

"You're a big girl now, Breezy, and big girls have their own rooms."

"I don't want to be a big girl!" she sobbed and ran downstairs.

This was the first change that upset Breeze, but many other adjustments soon followed. Once, Breeze's parents had ran out of milk, so JJ had the last bottle and Breeze was given water.

"That's not fair! I don't want water with my cookies."

"I know darling, but the milk's finished," her mother replied.

"But why can't we buy some more?"

"It's late now, and the shops are closed. I'll buy some first thing

in the morning, and you can have a big cup of milk with your breakfast, ok?"

"But I want milk now. It's not fair. Why does JJ get everything?"

As Breeze continued to complain, her mother became increasingly frustrated. "JJ's a baby. He needs it more than you do, Breeze." Although this was hard to hear, Breeze could accept her mother's point. But what she couldn't accept was what came afterwards. "Don't be jealous, Breeze."

Whilst Breeze knew that her mother was stressed at the time and didn't actually believe that her daughter was a spoilt, selfish child, she felt so guilty. She always did everything she could to be the best big sister ever and her mother regularly told her that she was doing a great job. She had never been called a jealous person before and never wanted to be called one again. Breeze didn't realise how much those words had affected her, but they had and continued to impact her as a teenager. From that day on, Breeze didn't complain when JJ, or anyone else for that matter, had something that she didn't, even when she was well within her rights to do so. Even when something was genuinely unfair. Like the times when she would say a correct answer in class, but the teacher would mistakenly praise another student for it. Or if she was the first in line but the dinner lady served someone else before her. The fear of being called jealous or being perceived as an unkind person would always stop Breeze from protesting, and she had never been accused of being jealous again.

***

Since winning the athletic heats, Breeze's newfound popularity had caused her friendship with Bella to deteriorate. Her friendship with Jayden however had blossomed and Chanel's jealousy towards them was the talk of the school. They would train together, meet up to walk through Victoria Park on Saturdays and text each other every day without fail. Breeze had gotten to know a different side of Jayden and was pleasantly surprised when she realised that beneath his charm and bravado, was a nature-documentary-loving, board-game-playing and vintage-video-game-collecting teenager, who was just as passionate about athletics as she was. She admired the way in which he looked after his younger sister, Tia, since his father died, and he felt even more responsible to make sure that she was always ok. Jayden also shared Breeze's love for MC Hammer, although he didn't let anyone else know that. Their friendship developed quickly and after a few weeks of bonding, Jayden asked Breeze if he could take her out for dinner.

The day of their first date had arrived (although Breeze preferred to call it their first meal, as 'date' felt too formal) and they both agreed that Uncle D's would be the perfect choice. However, as they walked towards the end of Roman Road and Breeze saw that half of her year group were there as well, she regretted her decision.

Jayden and Breeze were seated at their table and could hear Oga D, the owner of the Nigerian restaurant next door, and Uncle D arguing. Everyone in Aspire Academy knew how lucky they were to have these two restaurants in the area. They were both award-winning and recognised for having the best African and Caribbean cuisine in East London. They were also a popular choice for students because they had special meal deals for under-16s, a fact that Breeze had forgotten when she agreed to eat at Uncle D's that evening.

"Why is it so busy in here today, Jayden?"

"Tun' up Tuesdays. Have you never come here on a Tuesday, Breeze?"

"Only straight after school, not in the evening."

"Oh ok. Yeah, Tun' up Tuesdays is a vibe. Uncle D gets a DJ in and there's free fruit punch all night. They even have a non-alcoholic version for the youngers," Jayden explained.

Their conversation was impeded by a combative Nigerian accent. It was Oga D. "Would you turn down that bumba bumba, fire bun, ta rass music! You're disturbing my customers," he demanded.

"Look nah man, wha' 'appen to ya? Ya bright and brazen! Don't come up ina my shop with all ah dat nonsense. Ah *my* restaurant!" Uncle D yelled.

Their insults flew back and forth like cannons in a war zone. Eventually, their slander ceased, and the room became silent as everyone looked on in apprehension. They stared into each other's eyes before unexpectedly braking into uncontrollable laughter.

"My brudda!" said Uncle D.

"Yes oh!" Oga D replied.

"Don't forget to bring my jollof and suya later, na man!"

"Ah ah! This man and food. I said I will bring it, relax."

As they embraced each other, the DJ switched the music back on and the lively atmosphere was restored.

"Why do they always do that?" asked Breeze.

"They're best friends, you know," replied Jayden. "The other day Uncle D was telling me how they've been friends since Oga D came over from Nigeria in Year 9 and their teachers always used to say, 'Desmond and Dayo, stop arguing', but they always had each other's back."

"Well, guess not much has changed then."

"Trust. Anyway, what do you fancy?"

"Huh?" Breeze was overcome with embarrassment.

"To eat…"

"Oh… of course — to *eat, obviously*, that's what people do in restaurants, right?" she cleared her throat and chuckled nervously. "What else would we do? Dance? Imagine dancing at a dinner table instead of eating! That would be nuts, innit?" Breeze realised that she was overcompensating for her blunder and quickly composed herself. "Erm, yeah, I'll have the curry chicken meal with a side of plantain and a Sun Exotic tropical drink, please."

Jayden smirked contently. "Nice, nice. I'm getting jerk chicken with rice and peas, mac and cheese, coleslaw, plantain, festival, *and* dumpling. All washed down with a can of Ting. Big man meal, you see it! I'll go and order."

"Thank you," she replied. As he walked towards the counter, Breeze reprimanded herself. "Dance… really Breeze. Why? Just why? You alwa–" Her rant was interrupted by her acknowledgement of Bella walking into the restaurant. "Great. Just, great. Because things aren't awkward enough already."

"Hey."

"Hey."

Bella sat in Jayden's seat and Breeze felt her heart rate increase.

"You look nice, Breeze. You wearing makeup?"

"Yeah, just a lil'. I tried a ting."

"Tried a ting, fair enough. I thought you hated makeup and putting anything on your skin."

"Yeah, I do."

"You do... Ok. Looks good, though."

Bella's began to nervously tap her fingers and Breeze subconsciously mirrored her.

"This is a bit awkward, Breeze. I feel like we haven't spoken for months and it's only been three weeks."

"And two days... not that anyone's counting."

They briefly paused and once again, their trail of thought was identical.

"I miss you," they said at once.

"I'm sorry, Bella... I shouldn't ha–"

"Yo, Belly! You crashing our date?" Jayden interjected.

"Date? Oh, course... date. Erm, no, I just came over to say 'hi'. Enjoy your date." As Bella left the table and approached the counter, her heart became heavy; she felt as though she was losing her best friend. "Can I get a cheesy beef pattie and coco bread, please?"

Whilst waiting for her order, Bella eavesdropped on Jayden and Breeze's conversation.

"Food should be here soon, B."

"Thanks, J."

"*J?*" Bella muttered. "Since when?"

Jayden danced along to the music playing from his phone. "Listen, this new YC song bangs! When the beat drops, it slaps differently!"

"Yeah, it's catchy," Breeze spoke as quietly as she could, but Bella's hearing had always been extraordinary; she could hear every word.

"YC. Catchy? Wow, Breeze," said Bella.

"Wha' ya say?" replied the waitress.

"Sorry, I wasn't speaking to you," Bella explained.

"Then who ya ah talk to?"

"Erm – myself!" Bella chuckled as the waitress glanced at her from head to toe and went to serve the next customer.

Breeze and Jayden began to rap along to the song:
"Money, cash, coins and pounds,
Every day we're making rounds,
Stacking P, without a sound,
Rolling through these London grounds."
"Jeez, Breezy! What you know about these tunes!"
Bella was horrified. "This cannot be real. This can't be happening." Her sadness was swiftly replaced with rage and before she knew it, Bella was marching over to Breeze.
"What's happened to you? You hate YC!'
"He's all right, actually."
"Really? Really? He's all right. Please explain the meaning of what you just rapped."
Breeze stood up and tried to console Bella. "It's just about working hard to earn money. It's encouraging people to strive for success. What's wrong with that?"
"Wow. Really, Breeze?" Bella's voice grew louder. "Hard work? Success?"
"Chill out, Bella."
"Yeah chill out, Belly," Jayden echoed, "one day you'll be cool enough to know about YC too," he joked.
Breeze laughed uncomfortably.
"So that's funny, yeah? You're laughing at me with your new boyfriend now. You're a joke!"
"Joke? No, Bella. I'm just popular now. Must be hard for you to accept. Are you jealous?"
"Jealous!" Bella shouted, "Breeze! How could you even say that to me? Have I ever been jealous of you? I've always been your biggest fan." Her voice began to tremble. "I thought you were mine too." With tears in her eyes, Bella ran out of the restaurant.
At that moment, Breeze felt like her younger self being reprimanded by her mother. She remembered how crestfallen she was when she was called jealous. "Bella, wait!" Breeze began to follow her, but Jayden held her hand. "I *am* your biggest fan, Bell."
"Our food is here, Breeze. It will get cold… B." Breeze took a deep breath to compose herself and sat down at the table.

"Wagwan for that girl? She left without her pattie and coco bread!" said the waitress.

Oga D was walking towards Uncle D's to deliver his jollof rice and suya when Bella ran into him, knocking the food onto the ground.

"Look at what you've done! You children don't look at where you are going! It's very, very bad. You just–" Oga D soon realised who he was shouting at. "Bella? Is that you? What is wrong, my dear? You don't have to cry, it's just jollof. Uncle D is big enough anyway. He should be reducing his carbs! Don't worry about it."

"It's not that, Oga D." Bella struggled to speak. "I– she– she called me jealous!" she said as she burst into tears.

"Oh dear! Come, come to my restaurant. I can't stand to see you cry like this. Come and eat. You can have this meal on top of the house."

"You mean on the house?" Bella snivelled.

"Ah, ah. That's what I said, now."

"Oh, thank you."

As they entered Oga D's, Billy, the owner of the local chippy, noticed Bella's grief. "Cheer up, darlin', it might never 'appen. Listen, you're in the right gaff to turn that frown upside down! Don't get me wrong, bangers and mash will always have my heart, but this jello rice – I could eat it all day! It's a bit spicy though, cor blimey! But add a good old Supermalt, fresh out the fridge and you're good to go!"

"You mean jollof rice," Bella explained.

"Yeah love, that's what I said."

"Don't mind Billy," said Oga D, carrying a tray with enough food to feed Bella's entire family.

"Is this all for me? I can't finish it."

"Don't worry, you can finish it. You need to eat very well to stay strong with all that gymnastics you do."

"Athletics. I do athletics."

"Ah, ah. This girl. That's what I said. Come on, just eat what you can, and I'll give you a container for the rest. Tell Oga D what happened."

Bella alternated between eating her fried rice and her explanation of events. Oga D seemed to understand and did his best to advise her.

"I'm sorry, Bella. This is a *very*, very hard one. Hmm. Listen, friendships are not easy and sometimes we have our arguments. Look at me and Desmond. That man can drive me mad! Oh God! But he is my best friend. We have been through so much together. He is the godfather of my two boys and I'm the same to his daughter. We just get each other, and we always support each other. You know, every time after we quarrel, we always reconcile and break bread together. You know why?"

"Why?"

"Because we know that the friendship that we have is rare and is hard to find. When you find a friend that really understands you and who you can be yourself with. A friend you can trust. Oh! My dear, hold onto that person and work through your problems. That is too valuable to let go. Do you understand me?"

"Yeah. I guess so."

"Listen, there is a parable, from my village back home, which says when a lion roars, the village is filled with fear. They fear the violent and dangerous predator. However, his lioness and his cubs do not tremble."

Bella looked at him with confusion. "Oh so, the lion... it roars, and people are scared, but... I don't get it."

"My dear, the villagers are scared because they don't know the lion's heart, they just see a wild animal. However, the lion's family know who he really is, they see a loving protector. You know who Breeze truly is. Don't look at her as a villager would and see her roar, look at her as your best friend, and see her heart. Trust that her good heart will bring her back to you."

Bella nodded in agreement and smiled. "I get ya. Thank you, Oga D," she replied as she hugged him.

"Oh, no problem, my dear. I believe that you two will be friends again very soon."

"Really? We'll see. I've got to go now. If I don't get home before eight, Mum will cuss."

"Ok. Get home safe, Bella," said Oga D, handing her a bag full of takeaway. "Greetings to your mum and dad." He sat down with an expression of contentment.

"Oi mate," said Billy.

"Oh! What do you want now, Billy?"

"That story about the lions…"

"Yes…"

"Is that a real… what d'ya call it again… parable? Is that true, then?"

Oga D's eyes shifted from his left to his right. "It doesn't matter if it's real or not, as long as she learned the lesson, that's what's important, no?"

Billy's laughter was so loud that it woke the baby, who had just fell asleep in her mother's arms, sitting on the table behind him.

"Shh!" Oga D snickered.

"You're a legend, mate."

03.03.2017

Once upon a time, in what felt like a far, far away land, Breeze believed in fairy tales. Every time she read or watched one, she would imagine herself as the princess, waiting for her prince to arrive and whisk her off her feet. However, as she grew older, six to be precise, she became sceptical of the whole idea. Now Santa Claus she could believe in; she had visited his grotto and everything. But she had never seen a prince on a flying carpet and when she tried to fly her bedroom rug, it didn't end well for her. The concept of a long-haired princess in a tall tower also baffled her.

"It just doesn't make sense. Why would anyone build a tower so high? And why couldn't she just go down the stairs? Where were the fire exits?" Clearly a health and safety hazard.

But her final confirmation that fairy tales were make-believe was her first crush, Fai Wu. Fai had recently moved to England from China and joined Breeze's primary school in Year 2. Miss Flower asked Breeze to be his buddy and make him feel welcome, another responsibility that Breeze took very seriously. They played together, had lunch together and after a few days, Breeze even felt comfortable enough to introduce him to some of her insect friends. At the end of his first school week, Fai thanked Breeze for being a good friend. He told her that she was pretty and kissed her on the cheek, before running away, leaving a bashful Breeze standing in the playground. Many thoughts raced through her mind: "That's strange, why did he run away? ... I've never been kissed by a boy before... friends don't kiss each other... does that mean he's my... boyfriend?"

At the dinner table that evening, when her mother asked how her day was, Breeze thought it would be the perfect moment to share her news. It wasn't.

"I've got a boyfriend! He kissed me on the cheek!"

Breeze's father almost chocked on his drink as he spouted, "What!"

Her mother gently held his arm and whispered, "Calm down, honey."

"Sorry, um, what do you mean by that, Breezy?" he asked as his left eye began to twitch involuntarily.

Breeze's eyes started to well up and her lip quivered, "Am I in trouble? Have I been naughty?"

"No, no. Of course not, darling," her mother replied.

"So why is Daddy's eye doing that?"

"It's just my hay fever, don't worry about that. Tell Daddy what happened."

Once Breeze explained who Fai was and what had happened, her father calmed down. Her mother explained that Fai wasn't her boyfriend but was just a boy who was her friend. A concept that Breeze didn't quite understand.

The following Monday, as Breeze walked into school with her father, who was holding her hand a little tighter than usual, she saw Fai standing by the water fountain. She hugged her dad and rushed towards Fai, unaware that he was taking to Josie, a girl in their class, who has hidden behind the corner of the wall.

When Breeze got closer to Fai, she could overhear him. "You're really pretty," he said before kissing Josie on the cheek, but this time, he didn't run away. He held her hand and they walked to class together. Breeze couldn't articulate what she felt at the time, but she knew it didn't feel good. She knew that she didn't want to feel like that ever again. Without realising, from that day on, a shield guarded her heart. A shield that Jayden was now beginning to break...

***

Jayden walked to Lockley estate to take Breeze to Chanel's birthday party. He whispered words of encouragement to himself for the entire time.

"Come on, G. You got this, man. You *been* gettin' girls from day! Lily in Reception, Shanice in Year 6… She was leng, still! But obviously SATs and that; it was the wrong time for distractions. Even Jasmin in Year 7. This is light work, man!" His inducement was disrupted as he stumbled up the stairs.

"You all right there, hun?" said Tina, a resident of Lockley Estate.

"Yeah, yeah. I'm cool," he replied, brushing off the non-existent dust on his shirt in embarrassment. "This is the second floor, right?"

"Yes, hun. Doors one to ten are to your left and eleven to twenty are down that way," she answered, staring at him.

"OK, thanks… I'm going to number two so I'ma head this way, then."

"Aww! The Bassey's gaff. They're a lovely family, ain't they?" She noticed the flowers in his hand and her voice transformed into that weird voice people do when they're talking to babies. "You going on a date?"

Jayden chuckled nervously, "Um, yeah. Something like that. Anyway, nice to meet you. Have a good evening."

"You too, love," Tina replied as she stood and watched him walk towards Breeze's door. "Bless his little heart."

"Door two. Ok. Drip: on point. Flowers: all good. One last breath check. You're ready, my G." Jayden went to lift the door knocker but froze when the pressing question exploded in his mind: 'How many times do I knock?' "One knock isn't enough, three knocks is too keen. Two. Two should be cool, innit?" he thought to himself. When suddenly, he noticed a doorbell. "Why man! Why have a knocker *and* a doorbell? How's anyone supposed to know which one to use? Cha!" he complained. He paused and began to think intently. "What if the doorbell don't work, though? Ah this is long! Just knock the damn door, Jayden! You're moving mad!"

Breeze heard Jayden's voice outside and was keen to open the door before her father did. She swung the door open to see Jayden standing there, speechless as he looked at her.

"Hi, Jayden… ain't you gonna speak?"

"Sorry. Um, hi. You alright? You look… You look nice."

"Thank you. You look good too."

"Yeah?"

"Yeah."

"Thanks… I got you these, innit… flowers and that."

"Flowers and that, yeah?" Breeze beamed.

"Yeah, minor."

"They're beautiful. Thank you, Jayden."

Their conversation was interrupted by Breeze's father, who gave Jayden a firm and elongated handshake as he introduced himself and explained that he was a former boxer (he attended an after-school boxing club in Year 4). "Look after her, young man. I'll pick her up at midnight," he instructed, Jayden's hand still in his grip.

"Just like Cinderella!" Jayden joked, but Breeze's father did not appreciate his humour. He did not respond and stared into Jayden's eyes sternly. "Yes, Mr Bassey… midnight."

"Ok. Bye, Mum. Bye, Dad!" Breeze clutched onto Jayden's arm and lightly pulled him towards the door. "Let's go," she whispered.

Her father watched them from the balcony as they walked down the street. "My baby's going to her first house party… she's growing up… I don't like it."

"She'll be fine, honey," her mother said as she gently closed the door and ushered him into the living room. "Just think back to when we were their age. As long as Jayden behaves like the sensible teenager you were, Breeze will be fine, right?"

A moment of deep thought overwhelmed Mr Bassey. Gradually, his eyes widened, and he yelled, "That's it! She's not going! Party lock off! Where's my car keys, babe? Where are my damn keys?"

Mrs Bassey's laughter provoked him even further and she knew she had to settle him before he ruined Chanel's party. "Stop, babe. Breeze is a good girl and you know it. Don't humiliate her like that in front of all of her friends. She's got this."

"Hmm. Fine. Fine. Can I just sit outside the house in the car and wait for–"

"No, baby."

"But–"

"No."

"Fine. But I'm getting there before midnight. Trust and believe that."

Cautiously, Jayden looked behind him and was relieved to see that Breeze's father was no longer watching him. "Your dad's serious, innit. He don't play."

"He can be like that sometimes, but he's cool really."

"I don't blame him, anyway. I would be protective if I had a daughter like you." They smiled in unison as their eyes met each other, and the tense mood vanished. Whilst they walked to Chanel's house, Breeze and Jayden joked for the entire journey.

"And then she would rub so much cocoa butter on my face, telling me that it would last the whole day!" exclaimed Jayden, bending over as he let out a surge of laughter.

Breeze giggled at Jayden's overstated amusement. "My mum used to do the exact same thing! I used to be so shiny for the whole of primary school!" she replied.

"Trust me!"

Twenty minutes passed rapidly, and before they realised, they had arrived at Chanel's door. Jayden could sense Breeze's nerves. "Don't worry, Breeze. I've got you."

"I don't know about this, J. I've never been to a house party before and I hardly know anyone and–"

"Chill, B. If you want to leave, at any time, we'll leave. Just say the word. I've got you," he repeated.

"Ok. Thank you, J."

"It's all good. Just try to relax and enjoy the vibe. Should be lit."

Jayden rang the bell and began to dance like MC Hammer to lighten the mood whilst they waited for Chanel to answer. Breeze's laughter was so loud that Chanel could hear it over the sounds of Yung Coin blasting through her house as she approached the door.

Breeze tried to regain her composure. "Oh, hi Chanel!"

"Happy birthday!" said Jayden

"Yeah, happy birthday, Chanel. This is from me and Jayden," said Breeze, handing Chanel a card, which they had both signed, with a twenty-pound note in it.

They scuttled into the house with grins on their faces.

"Rah," said Armani, Chanel's best friend. "One card from the two of them... that's a proper couple move, boy!"

"Look at them, coming to my party together like to say he's not mine."

"Clearly he's not," replied Armani.

Chanel gave her a scowl of reprimand. "Listen, when you can, distract Breeze... I need to get him alone."

"Cool. Go get your man, girl!"

"Here, Breeze. I got you some fruit punch," said Jayden.

"Thanks, J." After one sip, Breeze winced and spat the drink out like a hosepipe, showering the floor. "Guys, there's alcohol in this drink!" Breeze declared as her peers stared at her for stating the obvious. "*Obviously* there's alcohol in it!" Breeze chortled, "I knew that. What else would we drink at a party? Capri-Sun! Ribena! Squash! Are we twelve? No, we're fifteen... Minor, right?" Once again, Breeze recognised that she was overcompensating. "Let me get something to clean this mess up. I'll be back in a sec!" She rushed to the toilet and poured her drink into the sink. "Ew! Alcohol's nasty! How can people drink this for fun?" She gathered the toilet roll and began to wipe off the punch on her trainers.

"Yo, you need to sort out your girl. She's moving mad," said Ade.

"Leave her alone, man. She's new to all of this and she's a bit nervous," Jayden disputed. "*And* she's not my girl... yet," he said with a playful smile.

"Yet! Is that you, yeah!" Ade shouted. "What about Chanel, though?"

"Ay, man. Why you shouting? Listen, Chanel's cool but the vibe ain't right. We don't have nothing in common. Like, the conversations are dead. *Breeze* now, she's proper. She's a proper nice girl, but we're still getting to know each other."

"I hear that. Early tings."

"Yeah, exactly. It's still early. Anyway, how you been, bro? Man like Ade Ade!"

"I've been here, G. Been a calm one today, still. Did you watch *Done Out 'Ere*? Oh my days! That show is too much jokes, I swear!"

"Nah, I don't watch them things. It's so dumb. I just caught up with *Tower Block Tales*. Now that show bangs! It's so deep, fam."

"Yeah, TBT's sick, still. Nice one to watch with the ladies and that; they be getting all emotional and *then* they be wanting a hug and that. Get me!"

"This guy. You're not serious. But ladies, yeah? Is that you? Who you chattin' to?"

"Man don't even wanna talk too much, but there's this one gal, innit. She's nice but she's so confusing. Like, she be acting like she's onto man but then she starts moving all mad. Airing my calls, acting like I'm annoying her and all that. It's long, fam."

"Acting. I don't think she's acting you know, bro. You be annoying me."

"Is it? Like that, yeah? Cool. Say no more. All good. No problem. Say less."

"Calm down, G! I'm joking. I hear what you're saying, though. Girls are different; they can be hella confusing."

"Trust me. Speaking of which, here comes your ting."

"I've got tissue!" Breeze announced as she re-entered the room and wiped the spillage. An unexpected transition from YC's latest hit, 'Mulla' to MC Hammer's classic, 'U Can't Touch This', sparked an excitement in Breeze. "No way," she said as she did the Running Man. "Come on, Jayden!"

"What is she doing, bro?" said Ade.

"Jayden! You love this song!" she yelled, for all to hear.

"Is it, Jayden? Is this your tune, yeah?" Ade teased.

"Nah, never! But you know how it is with girls – you've gotta act like you like the same things they do sometimes. Keep them sweet. You get me?" Jayden winked and muttered, so that Breeze couldn't hear him.

"Yeah, yeah. I hear you," said Ade as he slapped Jayden's hand in admiration. "You're a G, you know!"

"Breezy, stop, everyone's staring at you. Breeze!" Jayden pleaded. But Breeze was in her own world.

"Mum!" shrieked Chanel, full of fury. "Turn that off! I said no old people music. Stop embarrassing me!"

And just like a slapstick comedy, the DJ stopped the track, Breeze slipped on the remnants of punch and hit the ground like an infant learning to walk (legs in the air and everything...

ouch). There was an intense pause of silence followed by an explosion of laughter. Thankfully, Breeze found it just as amusing and began laughing too.

"Are you all right, Breeze?" asked Jayden, helping her up from the floor.

"Yeah! I'm fine."

"I love how you don't take yourself too seriously, B," said Jayden as their eyes met yet again and they smiled at one another, oblivious of their surroundings.

"Um, I should go and get some more tissue to clean that up."

"Yeah, yeah. Um, you should, actually. That's a good idea, yeah. Cool," said Jayden. His eyes followed her across the room until they were met with Ade's creepy stare. "Ah, move, man!"

"Aww. You two are bare cute, you know," Ade goaded.

"Shut up, man. Your mum's cute."

"Allow it, bro. You can't be complimenting man's marge like that. Lucky it's you, you know. Anyone else and that could never ever run. Trust me. It would be-"

"Yeah, whatever. Shh, man."

Meanwhile, Armani was in secret agent mode; she immediately noticed when Breeze had left the room. Her target (Jayden) was accessible and her mission ('get Chanel a bae') was activated. "Chan, She's in the toilet; Jayden's alone. Make your move, now!" Armani commanded. "I'll keep her in there for a bit."

"Thanks, babe. You're a real one."

Chanel tapped Jayden's left shoulder and then moved quickly to his right. "Hey J, you having a good time, boo?"

"Boo?" he said under his breath. "Yeah, it's a vibe, man. Good food, good music, couldn't ask for much more."

"That's what you think," Chanel whispered, with a look of mischief on her face.

"What?"

"Nothing... It's hard to talk properly in here, J. I can't really hear you."

"I can hear you just fine, Chanel."

Chanel began to mouth her words inaudibly.

"What are you doing?" said Jayden.

"See, you can't hear me, let's go somewhere quieter to talk."

"I'm waiting for Breeze."

"Come on, Jayden. It's *my* birthday! You can't speak to me for five minutes? I'm sure Breeze will be ok. Or does she need you to babysit her all night?"

"Three minutes," said Jayden. He reluctantly followed her to the passageway and sat on the staircase, unaware that Breeze was in the toilet underneath them. Armani obstructed the toilet door, locking Breeze inside.

"Hello!" called Breeze, struggling with the door. "Hello, I'm stuck in here! Can anyone hear me?"

Armani acted as though she was concerned. "Hi, are you ok in there?"

"I can't open the door. I can't get out!"

"Oh no!" she performed, rolling her eyes. "I'll get help right away! Just hold on."

"Ok, thank you."

Chanel had positioned herself next to Jayden on the stairs. "I've missed you, J. It feels like I hardly see you anymore these days."

"I've been about."

"Yeah, with Breeze."

"Yeah, she's cool."

"Since when!" Chanel huffed in exasperation. "Just because she won that race! Gosh! *Now* she's a 'bad gal'! Please. I've been bad from day... we both have. We're a perfect match."

Jayden began to stand up. "Um, I should go and look for Breeze, check she's ok."

"Oh, Breeze! Breeze! Breeze!" Chanel seethed. "I've had enough!" She grabbed Jayden's face, pulling him towards her and kissed him. Jayden pulled away, but it was too late. Armani had released Breeze from the toilet, seconds prior, just in time to see their lips unite. Instantly, Breeze was transported back in time, standing in the playground, watching Fai kiss Josie and the shield over her heart hardened again. Jayden noticed Breeze and leaped up hastily.

"I didn't kiss her, Breeze! She kissed me, I swear."

"You don't need to explain yourself to me, Jayden, it's cool. You're single, right?" said Breeze, failing to hide her disappointment.

"Exactly," Chanel interjected. "You ok, Track Girl?"

"It's Breeze."

"Yeah, whatever. That was quite a fall! It's my mum's fault for playing that dead music. I told her to save that for her old people friends," she continued, laughing insincerely. "Innit, Jayden?"

"Yeah, I — I guess so," he stuttered.

"Anyway, I think it's time to cut my *four-tier* cake. Red velvet, vanilla, lemon, and fruit cake. Fit for a princess!" Chanel couldn't supress her satisfaction. Linking arms with Armani, she walked away and whispered, "We did it, girl."

"Why do you do that, Jayden?" asked Breeze.

"What?"

"Pretend to be someone you're not."

"It's not like that, Breeze."

"It is! You love MC Hammer, yet you stood there and let Chanel cuss his music."

"Yeah, I know but..." he exhaled, "look, Breeze. I'm *Jayden* you know. The junior national champ for long jump. People respect me. They look up to me."

"And? The national champ for long jump can't listen to MC Hammer?"

"Exactly. Now you get it. I've got a reputation to keep. Only special people get to see that side of me. Like you. *You* know the real me," he said and held her hand.

"Wow. I appreciate that you feel comfortable to be the real you around me, but I can't be around someone who wants to fit in with the crowd so badly that he can't be true to himself... I should go." Breeze began to walk towards the door.

"Breeze, wait."

"You know... you and Chanel actually suit. You make a good couple. Take care, Jayden."

Breeze closed the door behind her. She immediately thought about Bella: their promise to spend this day together; her promise to be 'normal' when she liked a guy and tears flowed down her cheeks as she sent a text to her father and asked him to pick her up.

– 10 –

Sorry

From a very young age, Breeze did all she could to avoid conflict. She couldn't bear the feeling of being upset with anyone or when she knew that she had made someone else unhappy. She also disliked witnessing other people argue and couldn't help but intervene. Although her parents rarely argued, Breeze vividly remembers every time she overheard them when they did. They would often wait until Breeze and JJ were asleep, (or when they thought they were sleeping) and would play music to mask their voices. But Breeze quickly realised her parents' strategy. Once, Breeze heard a glass break and ran downstairs in tears into her mother's arms.

"Breeze, what's wrong? Why are you awake?"

"Why are you fighting, Mummy?"

Her parents looked at each other, disappointed that they had allowed themselves to be heard.

"We're not fighting, baby," said her father, "we just disagree about something and we're trying to understand each other."

"That doesn't mean you have to shout. You should speak nicely and use your inside voices."

"I know, you're right, baby." He picked Breeze up and placed her in his lap. "Daddy made a decision about something very important and didn't ask Mummy first."

"But that's not fair, Daddy. When I ask Mummy for a treat after dinner, she tells me to ask you too."

"That's true. You're right, Breeze," he replied, placing his hand on his wife's shoulder.

"I'm sorry, honey. I love you."

"I love you too, babe."

As they kissed, Breeze realised what she had done and enjoyed the feeling of being a peacemaker. "I did a good thing, didn't I? Can I have a treat, Daddy?"

"Yes, you did, but it's late, baby. But... ask your mum," he replied and grinned.

"Can I, Mummy?"

"Hmm. You can have a tiny treat; one spoon of ice cream," said her mother.

This day taught Breeze that sometimes people who love each other will argue, but they can always resolve their issues if they realise why they are wrong and apologise. From that day forward in the Bassey household, the rule was to never go to sleep without resolving an argument. A rule they hadn't broken since.

As she sat waiting for her dad, Breeze thought about this rule and was disappointed in herself for allowing so much time pass without making amends with Bella. They had never had an argument and Breeze missed her best friend.

***

Breeze's father arrived in 6 minutes and 37 seconds (Breeze was counting) and came out of the car, ready to erupt.

"What's wrong, Breeze? Why are you sitting out here alone? Have you been crying? ... Jayden! I knew it! Where is he? I'm gonna—"

"Dad, please. Let's just go. I just want to leave."

"Ok, sweetheart. Come on."

Breeze didn't speak for the entire car ride home and once they were parked outside of their house, her father asked her what had happened.

"It's all a mess, Dad!" she sobbed, struggling to get her words out. "I've been a bad friend. I cheated in the regionals; that's why I won. I've never cheated before, I just panicked. Then everyone was my friend out of nowhere. And I'm not gonna lie, it felt kinda nice. But then I called Bella jealous, but she's not jealous. She's my biggest fan, and I'm her biggest fan, and now she hates me, and I've been at a stupid party, with stupid punch and people I don't even know, and Jayden just cares about fitting in with everyone, and — and — MY LEG HURTS!" she wept into her father's chest.

"Oh, baby. Slow down, calm down… breathe," he replied, kissing her forehead. "It sounds like you've made some mistakes recently, but the good thing is that you're aware of where you went wrong. That's a great sign of maturity, Breeze. We all make mistakes, but what's most important is what you've learned from them and how you make it right moving forward." Breeze started to calm down and think about what her father was saying. "I've seen the friendship you have with Bella – that's special, that's rare and I'm pretty sure that if you're hurting right now, she's hurting too."

"So, what do I do, Dad?"

"That's *your* best friend. You know what to do."

She wiped her tears and pulled an expression of determination. "I know what to do!"

"That's my girl."

"Dad, can I stay at Bella's house tonight?"

"Hmm."

"Please, Dad. I need to make things right. I've got a plan."

"Ok, darling."

"Thanks, Dad!"

He reversed the car and headed towards Bella's house.

"Oh, Dad. One more thing…"

"Yes, Breeze."

"Can we make one stop, please?"

"Where?"

"Dominos."

Breeze's father smiled and asked, "Why do I feel like this plan of *yours* is going to cost *me* money?"

Breeze's father held the pizza, drinks, and Ben & Jerry's ice cream as Breeze rang the doorbell.

"I'm nervous, Pops. What if she doesn't want to see me? This was a bad idea – let's go home."

"Go where? I didn't spend this money and drive you all the way here for fun. Stop overthinking, Breeze. Just speak from your heart."

"Hey, Mr Balivo," said Breeze as Bella's father opened the door.

"Hi, this is a late visit. Come on in."

"You all right, mate. I think the girls need to have a chat," said Breeze's father as they entered the living room.

"I see. Bella! Bella, darling. Come downstairs, please. Someone's here to see you."

Bella hesitantly came down the stairs and was shocked to see Breeze and Mr Bassey.

"Hey, Mr Bassey... Hey, Breeze."

"Hi, Bella. Sorry to turn up unannounced. Breeze really wanted to speak to you."

It was silent. Their parents pryingly watched them, waiting for someone to speak.

"Um, perhaps we should give them some space," said Bella's mother.

Their parents left the room and stood in the hallway, pressing their ears against the door. Overcome with nerves, Breeze's began to fidget with her fingers and Bella subconsciously mirrored her this time.

"I'm so sorry, Bella. I should have never called you jealous."

"Did you really think I could ever be jealous of you, Breeze?"

"No, never! I don't know why I said it. I shouldn't have said it. I shouldn't have cheated either. I was so focussed on maintaining my title that I lost sight of what's important: being true to myself and to the people who mean the most to me."

"To be honest, it was hard for me to see you spend so much time with Jayden, but I should have never called you a joke. I'm sorry too, Breeze."

"I've missed you so much, Bella! I've spent a lot of time with people in our year group who I've never even spoken to before and it's been... different. Some of them are cool, but some of them are just so... so not cool, even though they think they're the coolest thing since hard dough bread. If that makes sense."

"Yeah, I get you."

"But none of them are you, Bell."

"I've missed you too, Breezy."

"Really? I thought you were done with me. I wouldn't have blamed you if you were."

"No, just because we had a bad moment, that doesn't take away the years of good friendship."

They were emancipated from the weight of their discord, and Breeze was ready to share her good news. "I got us pizza!" she said optimistically. "Well, my dad did … you know what I mean."

"What flavour?"

"Chicken and sweetcorn."

"Jalapenos?"

"Of course. And I got ice cream."

"Ben & Jerry's?"

"Obviously!"

"Cookie dough?"

"Come on, Bell. Rate me, please."

"Yeah, that was a silly question, really."

Their smiles of relief soon became amusement and Breeze bear hugged Bella.

"You know our parents are listening, right?" uttered Bella through Breeze's tight grip.

"Course they are! You can come in, guys."

"Aww, you two!" said Mrs Balivo, hugging them both.

"I knew you would figure it out!" said Mr Bassey.

"Thanks, Dad!"

"Yeah, thanks for the pizza, Mr B!"

"Group hug!" said Breeze as they huddled in a circle and squeezed for dear life.

"Ok, ok, can we eat now, please?" asked Bella. She grabbed the food and ran up to her bedroom. Breeze ran after her with the drinks and ice cream.

"Guess we're not all eating together, then?" said Mr Balivo woefully.

"Guess not, mate," Breeze's father replied. "Thanks for letting Breeze stay over tonight."

"No problem. I'm sure they've got lots of catching up to do."

"Yeah, I bet. I'm just glad they've worked things out. I'll pick her up in the morning, around 10. Is that all right?"

"Yeah, that's fine. Goodnight, mate."

"Goodnight."

"I'm stuffed, Breezy. Look at my belly!" said Bella, cradling her stomach.

"Stop that," Breeze chuckled. "Ah, it feels so good to be back, Bell."

"You sure? You wouldn't rather be with your *boyfriend*?" Bella teased.

"Jayden and I were just friends, Bell. He wasn't my boyfriend… it's a shame because there's more to him than the vain, popular athlete. He's really cool and has a good heart, but I can't chill with someone who can't keep it real, you know?"

"Yeah, I hear ya. I'm just messing with you, Breezy. I knew you would come back… You were like a lion, roaring to a village, but I wasn't scared because I know who you really are."

"What? O — k. I don't get it."

"I didn't at first either!" Bella giggled.

"Anyway, you must be tired because you're waffling. Night, night, Bell."

"Night, night, Breezy," she replied. As Breeze put on her silk bonnet and began to pull at the covers, Bella grinned and softly said, "You were right, Oga D. She came back."

– 11 –

Fit for Purpose

When Breeze completed preschool and was ready for 'big school', she felt nervous and excited at the same time. She was also unhappy because she could no longer spend the day with her brother at Rise and Shine Playgroup. On her first day, as she sat on the bus 15 with her father, Breeze rested her head on his arm, silenced by worry.

"I know it can be a little bit scary starting a new school, Breeze, but you will love it. You'll learn so many new things and you'll make loads of new friends." (Well, that's what he thought). "And before you know it, the school day will be over, and you'll be home again with JJ. And then you can tell us all about your day. How does that sound?"

Breeze sat up and gently nodded.

"And remember, your school is right next to my office, so I'll always be close by."

Her father's words comforted Breeze and after some time had passed, Breeze was telling her dad how much she loved her new hairstyle and counting how many ribbons her mum had managed to tie around her twists. She had twelve in total (I know, slightly excessive, but it was cute).

"This is our stop, baby."

They got off at Aldgate East station and began to walk towards Sir James Charles Foundation School. As they were walking, Breeze noticed a man sitting outside the train station. He winked at her, which she found frightening because her preschool teacher, Carol, always said that she should, "Never talk to strangers because that's stranger danger." She tightly squeezed her father's hand as they passed him. However, when Breeze saw the same man, sitting

*outside the same station and wearing the same clothes the next
day — and the day after that, it troubled her. He wasn't the scary
man who winked at her every morning. In fact, Breeze thought he
was a very friendly man and didn't understand why he was alone.*

"Daddy."

"Yes, my dear."

"Why is that man sitting on the street by himself?"

"He's homeless, Breeze. Some people don't have a place to live
and so they have to live on the street."

"But that's not good. He must be very cold."

"Yes, it is very sad, Breeze."

"But where's his family? Why doesn't anyone help him?"

"I don't know, darling."

"Can we help him, Daddy? Can he come and live with us?"

"We don't have enough space for him at our house, but how else
could we help him?"

"Um, I don't know, Daddy."

"Think about it, Breeze. What could help him if he's living on
the street?"

"Um… I know, a jacket to keep him warm!"

"That's a good idea, and what might he need at this time in the
morning? What does Mummy say is the best way to start the day?"

"Breakfast! Can we get him some breakfast, Daddy?"

"I think that's a great idea, Breezy. Let's go to the café across
the road."

"But how will we know what he likes?"

"Let's get him a ham and cheese toastie and a hot chocolate.
Everyone likes ham and cheese toasties."

*When Breeze's father handed her the toastie and drink, she
looked at him in dread.*

"It's ok, Breeze. We will go to him together, but it was your idea
to help him, so I think that you should give it to him."

*Breeze stood in front of the man and was lost for words. She
thought about how Carol had taught her to introduce herself when
she started big school.*

"Hello, my name is Breeze, what's your name?"

"Hello, Breeze, I'm Lance. Nice to meet ya."

Breeze looked up at her father for approval.

"Go on, baby, you're doing a great job."

"Lance, me and Daddy got you breakfast. I hope you like it."

"Oh, thank you very much. I'm so hungry. What did you get?"

"A ham and cheese toastie, and a hot chocolate with extra whipped cream!"

"Wow! You must have read my mind. Ham and cheese toasties are my favourite. Thank you, Breeze. Cheers, mate."

As Breeze watched Lance take a supersize bite of his sandwich, she was filled with delight. Her father told her how important it is to help others, and from then on, every Friday they would buy Lance breakfast.

On one occasion, as Breeze handed Lance his toastie, he placed a coin in her hand and said, "That's my magic penny. It was given to me by someone very special and I've held onto it until I met someone special enough to give it to. You hold it tight for as long as you need to, and when the time's right, pass it onto someone else."

Breeze grasped the coin and said, "Thank you, Lance."

She cherished that penny and whilst she didn't believe it was magical, she did believe that it brought her good luck at some of the difficult times in her life. When she turned 12 and got her first set of house keys, Breeze asked her father to put the penny in a keyring and attached it to her keys so that every time she unlocked the door to her home, she was reminded of how fortunate she was to have a place to live. She made a vow that when she grew up, she would help people in whatever way she could.

***

With Sports Day weeks away, Breeze and Bella had been training strenuously to prepare.

"I still can't believe this will be our last Sports Day in this arena, Breeze," said Bella as they gathered their bags and left the stadium.

"I know, Bell. I haven't fully deeped it yet. I'm trying not to think about it too much. This is one of the few places where I feel like I'm just *me*, you know? There's no judgement when I'm on the track. I can just do my thing freely ... I think it will hit me hard once I run in that stadium for the last time."

"Yeah, it's sad… but like Mrs B said, we've got to honour it and just celebrate the times we've had there."

"Yeah. It's true and we will. You want to come over to mine, Bell and chill for a bit?"

"Yeah, we can check out that new Netflix series I was telling you about."

"Which one, again? *The Misfits*?"

"Yeah, it looks really good."

Breeze and Bella were almost at the top of Limehouse Hill, just around the corner from Breeze's home, when they heard a woman cry out in despair across the street, "My baby! Help! My baby!"

"Oh my gosh, Breeze," said Bella, "her pram!"

Breeze watched the pram briskly roll down the hill towards the congested crossroad and her reaction was instinctive. Breeze's trainers began to glow as she sprinted after the baby. Her speed increased expeditiously and within seconds, Breeze grasped the pram by the handle. The front two wheels hung on the curb of the pavement as a lorry drove past, blaring his horn in condemnation. Bystanders looked on in disbelief and a wave of applause flowed through the street.

"Blimey! You've got some legs on ya, girl! Is the baby all right?" asked Tracey, the owner of the local café. Breeze delicately pulled back the blanket and stared at the pram in confusion.

"Baby? … A cat?" Breeze muttered.

Before she could comprehend what had just happened, Breeze was joined by Bella and the cat's owner.

"Oh, you saved her, my baby! Thank you," she said, stroking the cat's back. "She's a rare breed, a Peterbald. Only two weeks old. I haven't even named her yet. Thank you so much, sweetheart. How can I ever repay you?"

"Oh, it's fine, you don't need to repay me," Breeze insisted.

"Well, thank you once again. You're a special young lady. You saved my baby's life! The way you ran was remarkable. You're very talented!"

"You're a hero, Breeze! Here, you dropped your keys," said Bella.

Breeze was overcome with timidity, "Ah stop, guys… thank you."

"Breeze… hmm. I think that works, she looks like a Breeze, don't you think?" said the woman, holding up her cat like its name should really be Simba.

"Yeah, you're right. I think she looks just like Breeze, um, I mean, like *a* Breeze," Bella teased as Breeze looked at her from the corner of her eye.

"Well, that's it, then. Baby Breeze! In honour of her hero. I must dash ladies, have a fabulous day! Ta-ta! Say 'ta-ta', Breeze," she said, waving her cat's paw.

"Ta-ta — oh, you mean the cat… of course," Breeze replied. Bella burst into laughter. "You're not funny, Bella."

"I'm hilarious, and you love it! You actually said, 'ta-ta'! Wow, you're too much, you know. Baby Breeze and that. I see the resemblance, still."

"You done?"

"Yeah, for now. Seriously, though, well done, Breezy. That was proper sick."

"Thanks, Bell."

Breeze began to think earnestly when she noticed a homeless woman sitting outside Tracey's café. She looked down at the keys in her hands and eyes were fixed on her keyring with her lucky penny.

"One second, Bella. I've gotta do something real quick."

"Ok, cool."

Bella followed Breeze into the café as Tracey was serving another customer. "Here you go, Sir. One ham and cheese toastie and a hot chocolate with extra whipped cream."

"Beautiful! Thanks, Trace," he replied.

"What can I get you two ladies?"

Breeze was distracted by the man Tracey had just served. "Um…"

"Breeze?" said Bella.

"Sorry, sorry. I'm listening. It's just that guy… he looks… don't worry. Can I get a ham and cheese toastie and a hot chocolate too, please?"

"There must be something in the air!" Tracey chuckled. "It'll be about five minutes, love. Take a seat."

Breeze couldn't stop looking at the customer as he ate his lunch.

"Stop staring, Breeze, it's rude."

"Sorry, I know. It's just… I swear I know that man."

"Really? Then you should go and say 'hi'."

"Yeah, but I'm not sure, he looks different to how I remember. I can't see him properly, his hat's in the way. It's been ages since I've seen him… like, four years."

"Well, do you know him or not?"

"I think I do… I'm gonna go and say 'hi'."

"That's what I just said, Breeze!"

But just as Breeze stood up, Tracey called out, "It's ready, girls! You can have this on the house, love. You deserve it after saving that baby… cat."

"Thank you, Tracey!"

"That was delicious, Trace," said the customer. "You've got the best ham and cheese toasties in town, I tell ya! I've gotta go. I've left a tip there for ya. See ya later!" he said as he rushed through the door.

"See ya later, Lance."

"Lance…" said Breeze. "Lance!" Breeze ran after him and looked up and down the street, but he had gone.

"What was that about, Breeze?"

"I did know him, Bell… now he's gone."

"Sorry, Breeze, I'm sure you'll see him again."

"Who? Lance? Yeah, you will. He's one of my regulars. Anyhoo, enjoy!" said Tracey as she handed Breeze her order.

Although this wasn't Breeze's first time, it had been a while and she was still nervous as she approached the homeless woman. Fortunately, she knew just what to say.

"Hi, my name is Breeze. What's your name?"

"Esmeralda."

"Hi, Esmeralda. We got you a toastie and a hot chocolate. I hope you like it."

Esmeralda spoke very little English, but it was clear that she was grateful. She held her hands together like she was saying a prayer and bowed repeatedly.

"Have a good day," said Breeze.

"Have a good day. That was so cool, Breezy. We should do things like that more often."

"Yeah, we should… You know, today's really made me think. Saving the cat — seeing Lance again. That's what I should be using these trainers for, Bella. To help people; to do good." Bella began to smile at her best friend. "Why are you looking at me like that? Do I sound silly? I sound silly, forget it."

"No," Bella interjected, "you don't sound silly, you sound like… like Breeze again, the Breeze I know."

"Aww, softy Bella at it again! Last one to my house does the dishes!" said Breeze, sprinting up the hill.

"What! That's not even fair! Breeze! Come back!" Bella called pointlessly. "I thought you just said that you were going to use your kicks to *help* people," she grumbled and began to jog up the hill.

When Bella arrived at the house, Breeze had already changed into her tracksuit and was laying on her bed."

"That – ain't – even – fair," Bella panted.

"Yes, it is. Payback. You don't remember pushing me to the ground and running off at the arena?"

"That was months ago, Breeze!"

"Yeah it was, and now we're even."

"Hmm, well I ain't washing no dishes," said Bella, collapsing onto Breeze's bed.

"Yes, you are."

"No, I'm not."

"Yes, you are."

"Make me."

"Yeah? You sure about that?" Breeze grabbed a pillow and was just about to attack Bella with it when she noticed a light, radiating from underneath her cupboard.

"Too slow!" said Bella, striking Breeze with a pillow, but Breeze did not react.

"Bell — Bella, do you see that?"

"Don't try it! I'm not falling for that!"

"No, seriously. Look," Breeze pointed towards the corner of her room.

"Oh yeah. What's that coming from?"

"I don't know, Bell. I've never seen it before."

"Well … go and see what it is, then."

"No, you go and see."

"It's your bedroom, Breeze."

"Yeah, but – I'm scared."

"Are you joking?" Bella giggled. "What could possibly be scary in your own bedroom? Ah, fine."

Bella approached the cupboard and saw that the light was coming from inside the shoebox for Breeze's birthday trainers. "Here. Open it."

Cautiously, Breeze opened the box, revealing an envelope with a card in it. "That's weird, I didn't see that in here before."

"Read it."

Breeze opened the card and it said:

Dear Breeze,

Happy belated birthday! I'm glad that you like your trainers, they were custom-made especially for you! Now that you have mastered your trainers and realised their true purpose, to help others, you are ready to complete your first mission. If you succeed, you will help to maintain Aspire Academy's sports specialism and save your school's arena.

I am sure that you are aware of the Aspire Coat of Arms at the entrance of your school, outside Mrs Banjo's office. If you look at it very closely, you will notice that there are three medals out of four missing from it. These medals belonged to former students of your school who went on to become very successful athletes. They are invaluable. However, they were stolen over fifty years ago and despite the public scandal this caused and police investigations, no one has been able to retrieve them. No one until now. Breeze, you have the power to find these medals and return them to their rightful place. Your customised trainers will assist you. Although you have mastered the trigger points perfectly and are able to run up to 100 mph, you have not discovered the 'Boundless and Beyond' speed. This is activated when you click your heels together (sort of like Dorothy in The Wizard of Oz). Once activated, you will be able to run so fast that you will become undetectable to the naked eye.

How will you find the medals you ask? Good question. Enclosed in this envelope are four cards. You must solve the clues on each card to locate the medals. Then, with the help of your trainers, you will be able to get them in a breeze! (See what I did there?). Finally, the fourth card belongs the former athlete whose medal currently remains in the coat of arms. This athlete is the final piece in saving the arena. Once you retrieve the medals, return them to this person and your mission will be complete.

You're probably wondering who I am, and soon you'll find out. It's been years since you've seen me, but I've always been close by. I've watched you grow into a smart, brave, and kind-hearted person; I always knew that you would. Just know that I have a lot of faith in you, Breeze.

I know you must have many other questions, and I assure you that they will all be answered in due course. For now, rest assured in the gut feeling that you have had recently: that there's been something magical about the last few months. Discovering the trainers, the way they are destined for your feet, the power they give you. Everything has been leading to this moment. With the help of your best friend, Bella, you will save your school.

Good luck,
Your faithful friend.

P.S. one final tip: remember to follow the glow.

Bella and Breeze had a rare experience: they were both speechless. Minutes had passed and not a single word was spoken. They would look at each other and then the letter, followed by Breeze's trainers, and repeated this sequence, but they did not speak.

Bella was the first to break the silence. "Try it."

"What?"

"The trainers... Dorothy... click the heels."

"Are you joking! Don't you remember what happened the last time I clicked my heels? You called me Bambi!"

"Breeze, that's the only way that we will know if this is real. That this ain't some weird prank. Come on, if this is true, Breeze, if this card is legit, you could save our arena... Try it."

With trepidation, Breeze stood to her feet and looked to Bella for guidance.

"It's ok, Breeze. You've mastered them now. You don't need to run far. Just click your heels, run downstairs to the kitchen and back again."

"Ok. Just click and run."

"That's it, click and run."

Breeze clicked her heels and took her first stride. "Done it," she said.

"What do you mean done it?" replied Bella.

"I ran to the kitchen and back."

"No, you didn't, Breezy. Come on, stop messing around."

"Bella? You mean you didn't see me go and come back? … Oh my days! It's true. It works. This is mad!"

"No way! You're being serious. I wasn't watching properly, so I must've missed it. Do it again."

"Ok."

"Wait! Bring something back from the fridge so I'm one hundred percent sure."

"Cool but look really closely this time and tell me if you see me go."

Breeze clicked her heels and in a blink of an eye, she had returned holding a block of butter.

"Oh — my — days!" yelled Bella.

"Oh my days!" Breeze repeated.

"OH MY DAYS!" they both shrieked.

"You didn't see a thing, Bell?"

"Not a thing. I saw you take a step to go, and then before I knew it, you were back here holding butter like some doughnut! Of all the things, Breeze. Butter, you know. Not even a little juice or something."

"Focus, Bella. Forget about the butter! Bell, are you sure?"

"I promise, I didn't see ya. I just felt a…"

"Felt a what? … Bella?"

"A … breeze."

The gravity of this revelation pulled Breeze down onto her bed and she began to think. As the last few months replayed in her mind, she felt overwhelmed. "Why me? I don't want this responsibility. It's too much pressure. What if I flop? I'll let the whole school down."

"You're asking the wrong question, Breezy. Not what if you flop, what if you *succeed*? You'll save our training grounds. This is what you were saying earlier about using your trainers to help people. This is the perfect opportunity to do just that."

Breeze nodded in agreement. "You're right, Bell. You're right... Call your mum and ask if you can sleep over today."

"Why?"

Rapidly, Breeze's facial expression evolved from one of fear to one of purpose. "Because we've got some clues to solve."

The Legends of Aspire

"Right," said Breeze. "Munchies: check. Juice: check. Ice cream: check. Let's do this!"

"We need to eat more fruit, Breezy," said Bella as she shook her head in disgrace and placed another Malteser in her mouth.

"Well, Skittles are fruit flavoured; that should count for something. Come on, let's get started!"

"Ok. The first card says:

Medal One:
Belonged to Benjamin Bailey
AAP Class of 1920
Olympic Silver Medallist for Swimming, 200m freestyle (1924)
Clue no.1:
Located in a centre after his name's sake,
A martyr, an angel or call him a _____
Clue no.2:
If your items go missing it would be a shocker,
That's why we must keep all our things in a _____
Clue no.3:
Once a year, Ben went away,
To celebrate his own _____."

"Ok, so I'm guessing AAP stands for Aspire Academy Poplar," said Breeze.

"Yeah, I thought that too. I think the medal is in a place that's named after someone important."

"That makes sense, hence the 'martyr' and 'angel'. So, we need to find another word for martyr or angel that rhymes with sake."

"Hmm... sake, cake, make, bake, take, la—"

"Bell," Breeze interrupted, "are you just going to list all the words that rhyme with sake? That will take ages! Think of a word that rhymes with sake and has a similar meaning to angel. You know, like... Saint."

"That sounds about right, you know! Saint. So, a centre that's named after a saint."

Bella thought intently. "How about St George's Leisure Centre?"

"Hmm... that would make sense actually because they have nice swimming pools and Benji was a swimmer."

"She said 'Benji', you know."

"St George's... I swear that's near Shadwell?"

"Yeah, it is. Wait, let me check something." Bella typed Benjamin Bailey into her phone web browser. "Look, it says he was born in America but moved to England aged five and lived in Wapping. So, St George's would have been his local leisure centre."

"It must be there, Bell. Nice, clue two, I think that's locker."

"Yeah, defo. I was going to say that. You put your things in a locker. That one was easy. For clue three, it says here on Ben's Wikipedia page that he travelled to a different country each year for his birthday... that's funny."

"What?"

"Look at his birthday... 22.02.1904."

"Hmm, our favourite number, two... So, his birthday must be the number of the locker, right?"

"I don't think so, Breeze. It's too long. But... It could be the locker *combination*. Normally, combinations are three numbers on lockers."

"So, 22-2-04?"

"Yeah. That should do it."

"Ok. First card solved, Bell. Let's write that down so we don't forget."

Bella spoke to herself as she wrote the answers down, "St George's, in a locker, combination 22-2-04."

"That was easier than I thought it would be, Bell."

"Yeah, not bad. But let's not speak too soon."

"Ok," Breezed sighed. "Card number two says:

Medal Two:
Belonged to Bianca Baker
AAP Class of 1925
Olympic Gold Medallist for the 400 metre hurdles (1932)
Clue no.1:
A royal member of the south would live in this location,
But not diamonds, another gem would mark the grand occasion.

Clue no.2:
To honour idols, we tend to handout trophies, plaques, and all,
And here, they honour great success with this historic _____.

Clue no.3
Second in and second up, that's what you need to pick,
To find the medal that you need, just look behind this _____."

"Right — so — ok... Yeah, I have no idea, Breezy."

"This one is harder that the first. But I'm thinking that it must be in somewhere like a castle because it says a royal person would live there."

"Yeah. *Or...* a palace. Buckingham Palace!" Bella yelled.

"Why are you shouting?"

"I don't know."

"It can't be Buckingham Palace, Bell. There's no way we could get in and why would athletes' medals be kept there?"

"True. And it does say 'of the south' so it's probably in South London somewhere. Is there a castle or palace in South London, though?"

"Hmm... I don't know, Bell. What about the diamond part? The location must be linked to a jewel in some way. Maybe it could have the name of a jewel in it... one that's similar to a diamond."

"Like an emerald?"

"That's not like a diamond, it's green."

"Oh, so you think it would be something that looks like a diamond... like a cubic zirconia."

"Yeah, kind of, but that's not special enough. It should be a bit more regal." Breeze's trail of thought was diverted by a swift ray of sunlight that glistened on Bella's birthday earrings. "Swarovski crystals," she whispered.

"Crystals!" they exclaimed.

'That's way more like a diamond, Breeze."

"Exactly. Bell, type in castle in South London with crystals."

"That's a long shot but I'll try it... No, this is all irrelevant. Nothing to do with sport. Let me try palace with crystals, South London." Bella looked at her phone irritably. "Come on... That's it! Crystal Palace Sports Centre. It's in South London."

"Yes, Bell! What do you think for clue 2?"

"Where would you keep items that honour historic athletes? That rhymes with all? ... it must be a wall."

"That makes sense. Does it say anything about a wall in the stadium."

"Yep! 'Visit our historical wall, honouring outstanding British athletes.' So, the medal should be on the wall?"

"Or in the wall? If it was on the wall, then it wouldn't have been so hard to find for all these years."

"That's true, Breeze. Ok. Well, walls are built with bricks... brick rhymes with pick, right? ... kind of. So that must be the answer to the third clue."

"Yeah. So, second brick in and second up from the bottom of the wall."

"Left or right, though?"

"What do you mean, Bella?"

"In from the left of the wall or the right of the wall?"

"Good question. The clues don't give that away. I'm going to have to figure that out when I get there.'

"Breeze, we're sick at this! We should be detectives."

"Calm down, Sherlock."

"If I'm Sherlock, that makes you Watson. Yeah, sounds about right."

"You wish, mate!" Breeze laid down on her bed. "All this problem-solving is making me sleepy."

"Come on, Breezy, we're halfway there. Here's card three:

Medal Three:
Belonged to Brian Bennett
AAP Class of 1954
Bronze Medallist for wheelchair tennis in the first ever Paralympics (1960)

Clue no. 1:
Locating this medal will take a short while,
This stadium took not an inch but a _____.

Clue no. 2:
Back and forth, their rackets in hand,
The crowd would cheer as they watched from the _____.

Clue no. 3:
When he did not play, he watched others compete,
His year of birth marks the _____."

"I've got clue number one, Bell. We need to find a word that rhymes with while and begins with a consonant because the clue used the article 'a' rather than 'an' so the answer wouldn't start with a vowel. Ms Browne went over that today in our English lesson. So that leaves any word beginning with either b, c, d, f–"

"Breeze!" Bella interjected. "Are you joking?"

"What?"

"It's *mile*... as in 'give them an inch and they'll take a mile'. Ain't you heard that saying before?"

"Oh yeah, I knew that. Obviously. Was just testing ya. Nice one, Bella," said Breeze in embarrassment.

"I think the mile is for Mile End stadium."

"That makes sense because the clue says that the location is close to us and Mile End's down the road. For the second clue, I was thinking stands."

"Yeah, I think you're right. Clue number 3 should be seat, that rhymes with compete... kind of."

"Yeah, that makes sense. So, the medal should be on a seat in the stands. Or under one. Search Bryan Bennett's birthday, Bell."

"This is getting ridiculous now."

"What's wrong."

"Guess when he was born, Breeze."

"When? 22.02?"

"Yeah! 1938. It says here he was twenty-two years old when he won the bronze medal. Wait a sec, let me check something… I thought so. Bianca Baker has the same birthday too!"

"And their names all start with a B – just like us. That can't be a coincidence."

"This is getting more and more bookie, but I guess it will all make sense very soon."

"I hope so, Bell. Anyway, so the medal should be on, or under, seat number 1938."

"Yeah, the clue says the year of his birth, so it has to be. I'm assuming it will be in the tennis court stands, right?"

"Yeah, that would make sense."

"Ok, so," said Bella as she picked up her notepad and began to write. "Medal two: Crystal Palace Athletics Stadium, historical wall, second brick in and up from the ground. Medal three: Mile End Stadium, in the tennis court stands, seat number 1938."

"Actually, 1938? Nah, that's too long of a number. Unless… wait let me check the layout of the stadium. Yeah, I thought so. It should be in block 19, seat number 38."

"You sure, Breeze? How d'you know it's not block 38, seat 19?"

"Hmm. No look, it can't be, there's only 20 blocks."

"Ok. Let me write that down."

"One more card left, Bell!"

"I know! Ok, Medal Four:
Belonged to Beverley Banjo
AAP Class of 1993
Olympic Silver Medallist for triple jump (1996)

Clue no.1:

An injury in '99 would end her Olympic features,
She left the world of sport for students and became a _____.

Clue no.2:
Here she found another job in which she could inspire,
And now she leads her former school, the children of _____.

Clue no.3
To save your school, you should by now know right where you should go,
Take all this information and head straight to Mrs _____."

"BANJO!" screamed Bella and Breeze in disbelief.

"Beverley? That's her name? She doesn't look like a Beverley. Hmm, Bevs and that," questioned Bella.

"You said 'Bevs', you know. Anyway, forget that, Bell. She was an athlete! An Olympic Silver Medallist! That's so sick!"

"I know! I knew Mrs B had some sauce in her! So why was she speaking like that in assembly the other day? Why is she letting them take our arena away from us?"

"I don't know, man. It doesn't make sense. She went to Aspire when she was a kid, she should know how much it means to the school."

"Maybe after her injury she didn't care about sport anymore."

"Nah. That don't sound like Mrs B. She's made sport such a big part of our school for years, she wouldn't just give up so easily. Check her birthday."

"Surprise, surprise, 22.02.1977. So, they all have the same birthdays and 'B-B' names."

"Wow, she was born in the 70s. That's mad... Did they even have colour TVs back then?"

Breeze's mother knocked on the door and walked into her bedroom before B Squared could invite her in. "Dinner's ready, girls. Rice and stew, fresh off the pot!"

"Ok, Mum, we'll be down in a minute." As her mother closed the door, Breeze began to grumble, "Yesterday we had pasta and stew, today we're having rice and stew, tomorrow, I bet we'll have spaghetti and stew. Not every day stew, man!"

"Stop moaning," Bella giggled. "Your mum's stew bangs. Plus, you should appreciate her cooking for you, Breezy."

"I do, I do. Just the same thing almost *every day*, you know? Anyway, on Monday, straight after school, we need to see Mrs Banjo and tell her what we know."

"That's *so* far away, Breeze. It's bad enough that we have to wait for the whole of Saturday *and* Sunday. Can we just go into school a bit earlier on Monday and see Mrs B first thing in the morning? I couldn't last the whole school day."

"Good point, I don't think I could bear that either. Ok, cool."

"Breezy."

"Yeah."

"We're a pretty sick team, you know."

"Come on, Bella! Dream team, mate. We bodied it today!"

Breeze and Bella did their handshake and went downstairs for dinner.

– 13 –

Mission Impossible

"You took your time," said Bella impatiently as Breeze approached the school gates at 8:03, three minutes later than they had agreed.

"Sorry, Bell. Mum was having a moan cause I left a plate in my bedroom. I don't even remember doing that, you know. It was under my bed. That's not like me, but why was she looking under my bed in the first place?" Breeze sighed.

Bella thought back to Friday when she stayed over at Breeze's house and remembered hiding her plate to decrease her washing up duty. "Ah — don't worry about that. Anyhoo, we still have twenty-five minutes till period one, let's go."

As Bella walked towards the automatic doors, they didn't open, and she collided with them. "Ouch!"

"Are you ok?" Breeze giggled.

"Yeah, I'm fine."

"Girls, no entry to students before 8.15," said the caretaker.

"Oh. Please let us in, Bossman. We have an important meeting with the headteacher. It's *really* serious." While Bella pleaded, Breeze tried to read the name on his cap, but it was washed out. She managed to decipher that it began with an 'l' and ended with an 'e'.

"Fine, I'll let you in. Only because I trust that you're both responsible and honest girls."

"We are. Thank you, Boss!"

"Thank you!" said Breeze.

They hurried through the doors, but Breeze became uneasy as they got closer to Mrs Banjo's office. "Wait!"

"What now, Breeze?"

"We can't just walk into her office like this, we haven't planned what we're going to say."

"We don't need a plan, Breeze. We'll just tell her about the letter and the trainers and your power and the clues and– "

"Bella! We can't say all of that, she'll think we're crazy. She won't take us seriously."

"Hmm, true... Ok, we can leave out your trainers for now and just start off by asking about the coat of arms."

"That's better, then we can tell her that we can find the medals. Cool."

"You ready now?"

"Yeah, I'm ready."

"Thank God for that! Only nineteen minutes remaining," said Bella as she knocked on the office door.

"Stop counting down, Bella. You're making me nervous," said Breeze, nudging Bella. Bella nudged back.

"Morning ladies," said Mrs Banjo. "Come in. To what do I owe this pleasure?"

Breeze and Bella smiled anxiously as they entered her office, still elbowing each other.

"Morning, Mrs Banjo," said Breeze.

"Morning, Miss," said Bella.

"Take a seat. What can I do for you?"

Breeze looked at Bella. Bella looked at Breeze. Breeze tilted her head to the side and widened her eyes, prompting Bella to speak. Bella mirrored Breeze.

"Is anyone going to speak? Or did you plan on just performing a mime?"

"Uh- no. I mean yes. I mean no to the miming and yes to the speaking," Breeze stammered.

"Sorry Miss, it's Monday morning and we're still half asleep!" Bella jested. "One of those coffees should do the trick!" said Bella as she stood up and began to walk toward Mrs Banjo's kitchen.

"Bella!" Mrs Banjo cautioned.

"Too much?" Bella whispered to Breeze.

"If you don't sit — down," said Breeze, clenching her teeth.

Bella slowly returned to her chair. "Sorry, Miss."

"Girls, I'm very busy at the moment, so if you don't have anything sensible to say—"

"No, we do, Miss," Breeze insisted. "I'm sorry, we're just a bit nervous. We wanted to ask you about the Aspire coat of arms."

"Yes, what about it?"

"We've noticed that there are some gaps in it, like something's missing."

"Yes, well-spotted," replied Mrs Banjo. "Those gaps that you noticed held medals of previous Aspire students who became athletes and competed in the Olympic and Paralympic games."

"*Really!*" Bella acted. "That's very interesting. We had *no* idea!"

"Yes, I wouldn't expect you to. You weren't even born when these athletes competed."

"So where are the medals now, then?" asked Breeze.

Mrs Banjo sighed deeply, "They're gone."

"*Gone!*" Bella shrieked, rising from her seat once again.

Breeze looked at Bella like a mortified parent with a child who's having a tantrum in the middle of a supermarket. "Sit – down," she muttered.

"Yes," Mrs Banjo continued, "they were stolen over fifty years ago, and the police were unable to find them."

"That's so sad, Miss," said Breeze.

"Very sad, indeed. Our coat of arms was created to honour those legends and inspire students in our school to go for their dreams. I remember learning about those athletes and how proud it made me to be an Aspire student when I was a child," replied Mrs Banjo.

"You went to this school as a child?" Bella asked.

"Yes, I did. They were the best years of my life, which is why I came back to work here."

"So why are you allowing our arena to be taken away?"

"Allowing? Do you think this is my decision, Bella? I'm just as disappointed about all of this as you are. Sport is what has made AAP special for decades. It's what I loved most about the school when I was a student here." Mrs Banjo became tearful. "Without sport, Aspire Academy just won't be the same. That's why I've decided to step down as your Principal; I refuse to play a role in implementing the new changes the founders are proposing."

"But Miss, there must be a way to fight this. You can't just give up," said Breeze.

"I have tried my very best, but some situations are beyond my control."

Breeze and Bella looked at each other and nodded in determination.

"What if we said we had a way?" said Bella.

"A way to do what?" Mrs Banjo replied.

"To save the school's arena."

"Bella, there's nothing you can do."

"Miss, what if we told you that we know where the medals are, and we could get them back?" Breeze said.

"Breeze, those stolen medals were a huge scandal. The police conducted extensive investigations for years to find them but couldn't. There's no way you two could find them. It's an impossible mission."

"Tell Tom Cruise that," said Bella, "or Star Girl."

"Miss, I know it's hard to believe, but Bella and I have found the medals; we know where they are. You've always taught us to believe: 'aspire, believe and achieve', that's what you've always said. Well, we need you to believe in us now, Mrs B. We've really found them, and we're going to get them and bring them back to our school, where they belong," Breeze explained.

Mrs Banjo was filled with hope. "If what you say is true — *if* you have truly found those medals, that could be just what I need to persuade our founders to maintain our sporting specialism and keep our arena open… it would provide us with the finances that we need to sustain the arena for decades, but–"

"But what, Miss?" said Bella.

"It's too late. The Chief Executive and founders are meeting here tomorrow to sign the final agreement."

"What time?"

"3:15."

"We'll have the medals back here by then," said Bella.

Breeze looked at her best friend in terror. "Bella?"

"We can figure it out, Breeze. We'll come up with a plan. You can do this."

Breeze was reassured and confidently replied, "We can do it, Mrs B. 3:15, on your desk."

"Hmm... Ok. If you get me those medals, I'll do the rest," said Mrs Banjo.

"Sounds like a plan! ... Um, Mrs B?" said Bella

"Yes."

"Wait a minute... There's still one medal left in the coat of arms."

"Yes, there is," replied Mrs Banjo tensely.

"Whose medal is that?"

"Um, that was won by another former Aspire student who used to do the triple jump, but focus on the other three medals for now, eh?"

Bella smirked and winked at Mrs Banjo. "Ok, Mrs B."

Mrs Banjo winked back and suddenly, Breeze and Bella noticed something unusual about her.

"Miss B, your glasses."

"What about them, Bella?"

"They're glowing."

"No, they're not."

"*Yes,* they are," Breeze objected.

"You can see it too, Breeze?"

"Yes, Mrs B. It's hard to miss!"

"Impossible," whispered Mrs Banjo.

Their prolonged silence was broken by the piercing school bell.

"Right, ladies! Off to period one! Good luck and let me know if you need anything between now and tomorrow's meeting," said Mrs Banjo, hastily leading them to the door.

"Thanks, Miss, we will," said Breeze. The girls scurried out of the office and ran to their science classroom, desperate to avoid a scolding from Mr Begum for being late to his lesson. They failed.

"Stop, stop, stop, stop, stop. Stop right there!" Mr Begum commanded, holding out his wooden one-metre ruler to obstruct their path.

Bella attempted to plead their case. "Sorry, Sir," she said, "we were with Mrs Ba–"

"You *were* somewhere else, when you should have been *here,* approximately two minutes and twenty-two seconds ago. That's one-hundred and forty-two seconds of learning you have lost. One-hundred and forty-two seconds that you cannot get back. But! There is hope. Thankfully, life presents chances… solutions. You can give me back the time that you owe me. You know how?"

The students of Aspire had endured this speech many times before and knew exactly what to expect next.

"Yes, we know how… de–"

"Don't interrupt me, Breeze. Please and thanks. You can give me back the time in…" he would always pause dramatically before yelling, "DETENTION!"

"But–" Bella protested.

"In the words of Florence Nightingale, 'I attribute my success to this: I never gave or took an excuse.' No excuses!"

"What's he on about, Breeze?"

"I ain't got a clue, Bell."

"Twenty minutes, two-hundred and twenty seconds!" Mr Begum exclaimed.

"But–" Breeze interjected.

"Each minute, each second multiplied by ten. You know the rules. Lunchtime or after school?"

"Lunchtime, please," Breeze replied on their behalf.

"Good choice! Now open your textbooks to page fourteen and answer the fifty questions in silence. We will go through the answers if there's time at the end of the lesson. Please and thanks."

"*Fifty* questions!" Bella grumbled. "So much for the precious learning that we missed. I could do this by myself at home!"

"Excellent idea, Bella! Year 10, you must complete the fifty questions on page fifteen as well for homework."

Bella slouched in her seat with a look of remorse as the whole class glared at her, including Breeze.

"How did he even hear that?" she whispered to Breeze.

"He hears everything," Breeze whispered back.

"That's right, Breeze!" Mr Begum commended.

After school, B Squared met at the mini pond to devise a plan for how Breeze would get the medals the next day.

"Right!" said Bella, pulling out an A3 sheet of paper with a timeline she had sketched on it. "I think I've figured out how you can get each medal throughout the day tomorrow."

Breeze stared at Bella in wonder. "Bella, how? When did you do all this?"

"In History. I was supposed to be creating a timeline of women's rights in Britain and the Suffragettes movement, but I couldn't concentrate. I couldn't take my mind off the medals. Don't worry, I'll catch up with the work, after we complete this mission. Can I continue with the plan now?"

"Go ahead, Bell."

"So, as I was saying, there are three windows of time throughout the school day when you can go and get the medals: break time, which is 25 minutes; lunchtime, which is 45 minutes and then after school, between 3 and 3:15, so 15 minutes. Now, it would make sense for you to get Bianca Baker's medal from Crystal Palace at lunchtime because it's the furthest away and get Benjamin Bailey's medal from St. George's at break time. Brian Bennett's medal is only in Mile End Stadium, with the trainers, you could be there in minutes so that should be the last medal you go for. We have Maths last lesson and Mr Fraser is calm so I'm sure he'll let you leave a little bit early if you say you're bursting for the toilet or something. That should give you enough time to get to Mile End Stadium, find the medal and be back before the founders arrive. I've written the details of each location and where to find each medal on the timeline, I think I've thought of everything. What do you think?"

"Seems like you've got it all figured out. Guess it's down to me now," Breeze sighed.

"You can do this, Breeze. You've just got to make sure that you're aware always aware of the time."

"Yeah. I think I will be fine. I have to be. This is for our Academy."

"Now you're talking! I'll be here to help you out as much as I can. I've got you, Breezy."

"Got you too, Bell."

"We should go home and get some rest; it's a big day tomorrow."

Breeze and Bella left the pond, unaware of the rustling in the bushes behind them.

"Is the coast clear?" said Chanel, desperate to avoid being seen.

"Yeah, they've gone," Ade replied, helping Chanel out of the sea of leaves.

"I thought you said no one knows about this place! You idiot! Imagine if we got caught. Imagine if people found out about us!"

"Well, we didn't get caught. And don't worry, I don't want anyone knowing about us either."

"Good," Chanel snapped, "you better not tell anyone, especially Jayden."

"You're jokes!" Ade snickered. "Jayden don't want you!"

"Jayden doesn't know what he wants… yet."

"What, and you do?"

"Yes. I want Jayden. My baby love."

"Baby love, yeah? So why were you just lipsin' my face off?"

"Oh please! Get over yourself! You wish I was. You're just a bit of fun… for now."

"You keep telling yourself that, Chan. In a bit."

"Ade, wait! What are those two up to?"

"I don't know. I don't really care to be honest."

"Did you hear what they said about bunking school? Hmm… I'm telling."

"Ah Chanel, 'low it man. Don't be a snitch."

"It's not about snitching. I'm concerned for their safety. They're planning on leaving the school premises during the school day; I think the school should know that, really."

"Whatever, Chan. Why do you have to be so mix-up?" said Ade as he walked towards the playground.

Chanel began to think about how she could get Breeze and Bella into trouble and her face lit up with excitement. "Whatever you're planning girls, I will end it."

14

The Aspire Coat of Arms

English was a lesson that Breeze and Bella thoroughly enjoyed. Ms Browne was one of their favourite teachers, and they particularly liked how she would spark debates within her lessons, linking their English topics to important issues within society. However, today was not the day for *A Midsummer Night's Dream*. Break time was fast-approaching and B Squared had one topic on their minds.

"I want us to explore that famous line in Act One Scene One: 'the course of true love never did run smooth'. It can be interpreted in various ways," said Ms Browne, ambling around the classroom. "One can argue that Lysander is reassuring Hermia and is optimistic because he believes that although the love they share will present obstacles, it will ultimately triumph. Alternatively, you could argue that he is a desperate man, who has just been publicly insulted by Egeus. Perhaps, he is trying to console *himself*, as well as Hermia, with the belief that things will work out for them. Very interesting, right?"

"Mm-hmm," Breeze hummed passively.

"But does Egeus have a right to choose his daughter's spouse? Arranged marriages are currently happening all over the world and many are successful. As her father, surely, Egeus should know what is best for Hermia and have her best interests at heart? *Or* is this an example of harmful patriarchy? Does forcing someone into marriage violate their human rights? Is this acceptable in our modern society? — Anyone?"

"Um, I don't know," said Chanel. "I'm a daddy's girl and he buys me everything I want, like this Chanel handbag and these

Prada shoes, so I wouldn't want to upset him because he might stop giving me all these expensive gifts, you know? But like, I am an independent woman too, and I do what I want, when I want, so if I wanted to marry someone like… I don't know… Jayden!"

Instantly, Jayden began to have a coughing fit.

"Are you ok, Jayden?" asked Ms Browne.

"Yeah, I'm cool, Miss. Sorry."

"Yeah, like I was saying," Chanel continued, rolling her eyes, "I would marry who I wanted, and my dad would just have to accept it. But if he didn't like it, my man would be rich anyway, and would buy me all the Chanel I could ask for! So, I'll be good regardless," she giggled.

"Says the independent woman," Bella mumbled.

Chanel kissed her teeth and continued, "I don't know, Miss. That's a hard one… really deep question."

Attempting to raise the tone of the discussion, Ms Browne looked to Breeze to provide a more thought-provoking response. "Breeze? Your thoughts?"

Breeze sat up in her seat like a child in Reception, her back uncomfortably straight, and began to formulate an answer based on the parts of the lessons she was able to remember. "Um, love. Love is a — complexed emotion. An abstract noun. We cannot hold love with our hands… but it can hold us."

"Wow," said Ade, clicking his fingers like he was in a jazz bar.

"And um, patriarchy is an outdated structure used to restrict and oppress women. But that guy… Egeus, he ain't all bad. I think he wants what *he* thinks is best for his daughter but he's going about it in the wrong way."

"That was deep," said Ade.

"Deep it was," said Ms Browne, smiling at Breeze. "Right, Year 10, summarise your thoughts on this quotation, analysing Shakespeare's use of language and referring to the context of Elizabethan England. You have ten minutes until break time, and I expect at least one analytical paragraph by then. Off you go!"

"Ten minutes!" Breeze whimpered.

"You're all good, Breezy. First stop is St George's, remember you've got twenty-five minutes to get there, find the medal and bring it back. Have you got the timeline I gave you yesterday?"

"Yep, it's here, in my pocket."

"Perfect."

"Yeah, I've just got to change into my trainers, then I'm ready to go."

"Cool, as soon as that bell goes, run to our spot, change and go. I'll be there waiting for you when you get back."

"Girls, can we get on with the task, please?" said Ms Browne.

"Sorry, Miss," they replied and started writing frantically.

Seven minutes had elapsed, and Breeze had completed her analytical paragraph.

"How do you write so much so quickly, man?" said Bella, leaning over to copy Breeze's work.

Breeze's attention was fixed on the clock and she didn't reply. She discreetly wore her hoody, zipping it all the way up to conceal her school uniform, and cleared her desk. As the clock handle made its final round to mark 10:30, Breeze subconsciously adopted the stance of an ambush predator, anticipating its target, ready to launch an abrupt, surprise attack.

"Twenty seconds," she said, sliding her chair back, her knees at a 90-degree angle, one leg in front of the other. She started to count down, "Ten, nine, eight…"

At this point, Bella was also filled with tension. "Good luck, Breezy."

Breeze gave Bella a thumbs up and continued counting, "Four, three, two…"

Immediately, Breeze shot up and rushed through the door. "Thank you, Miss!" she cried.

Ms Browne's perplexity was shared with the rest of the class as they gathered their belongings and left the classroom.

Bella power-walked in pursuit of the pond, but Ms Browne had some concerns. "One moment, Bella!"

She turned around slowly like a felon on the run, finally caught by the law. "Hey, Miss. How you doing? Great lesson — love a bit of Shakespeare; cheeky midsummer nightmare, and all tha-"

"Bella, what's going on with Breeze? Is she ok?"

"Breezy? Of course," Bella chuckled nervously, she lowered her voice and moved closer towards Ms Browne. "Between you and me, Miss, she had a dodgy curry yesterday; been on the bog all night. I told her not to come in, but she was like, 'No, no, no, I'm fine now, I can't miss English with Ms Browne.' But that's Breeze, right. It's kind of funny really! Anyway, I better go and check on her, make sure no one's teasing her in there and spray a little Impulse if needed. You know what I'm saying? See you later, Miss!"

Bella dashed through the door, leaving a suspicious Ms Browne seated at her desk. "These teenagers," she said.

At the pond, Breeze had changed into her trainers. With a glance over both of her shoulders to check that the coast was clear, one click of her heels and a powerful stride, she was off. She arrived at St George's Leisure Centre in under three minutes.

"Hi there, my name's Sally. Can I help you?" said the assistant.

"Hi, Sally, um, yeah I need a locker — please. Can I have a locker, please?"

"A locker for which facility?"

Breeze looked at Sally vacantly. "Huh?"

"Are you using our gym today or our studio or the swimming pool, or—"

"Swimming!" Breeze cried. "I'm going swimming."

"Ok, so our swimming pool is on the first floor and the lockers are located outside the changing rooms. You need a pound coin to open them and you can choose any vacant locker that you want. Except one."

"Except one?"

"Yes, one locker is jammed shut. It's been jammed for years and that's the only locker that needs a combination to open it, but no one knows what it is!" Sally chuckled and Breeze pretended to find it funny too.

"That's strange!" Breeze performed, before abruptly adopting her serious tone of voice. "Where's that locker?"

"I don't know, but it won't be there for much longer. My manager's getting it cut out and replaced today. Should be happening any minute now."

"Of course, that would be happening today," Breeze muttered under her breath. She glanced at her watch and realised she had lost ten minutes of her time. "Really? Ok, well thanks for all the information, see you later."

"Wait, excuse me, you need to pay for–" As Breeze walked away from the counter, Sally noticed that Breeze was wearing a school skirt. "Excuse me!" she yelled sharply.

Breeze detected her change of tone and returned to the desk. "Sorry, I didn't hear you," she replied.

"Shouldn't you be in school? It is forbidden for children use our facilities during school hours unless they are here with their school."

Breeze's felt her heartbeat rapidly increase and the palms of her hands become moist. She heard a group of students standing on the staircase. One pupil from this school approached the counter.

"Can I buy a pair of goggles, please?" he said.

"One moment, darling, I'm just dealing with something."

"I'm with this school!" said Breeze.

"*Really*? They arrived ten minutes ago."

"Yeah, I know. Uh, I had a dentist appointment, so I was late. My mum just dropped me off."

"Hmm, really? So what school are you from?"

"Huh?"

"What's the name of your school?"

Breeze noticed the badge on the student's blazer and recognised it instantly. "St Charles Academy."

"Young man, do you know this student?"

He looked at Breeze and she pleaded him with her eyes.

"Um... yeah, yeah."

"What's her name?"

"Huh?"

"I feel like a parrot today. It's a simple question. What – is – her – name?"

"Um, Shakeisha."

Breeze's eyes widened as she looked down at her trainers to avoid making eye contact with Sally.

"Hmm. Well hurry up *Shakeisha*, and get changed, your school's lesson starts in five minutes. Here are the goggles, young man. That will be ten pounds, please."

"Ten pounds, you know! Teef," he grumbled as he handed Sally the money and selected the silver pair. "Come on, Shakeisha, let's go!" he said, bending his arm for Breeze to link hers with it.

Breeze could feel Sally's eyes burning a hole in her back as she watched them walk away. "Don't look back," she said, "just keep walking." When they reached the first floor, Breeze let out a sigh of relief. "Thank you so much!"

"No problem. James. My name's James."

"Thank you, James... But really, Shakeisha!"

"It was the first name I could think of, it's my grandma's name."

Breeze began to laugh, but James failed to see the joke. "Oh, her name is Shakeisha, for true... she sounds like a G."

"She is."

Breeze looked at her watch. "Ten minutes left! I've got to go! Nice to meet you!" she said, running to the changing rooms.

"Wait! I didn't catch your name."

"Breeze!" she yelled as she ran.

"Breeze, yeah. Ok. Bye, Breeze," said James, grinning as he watched her go.

At the end of the corridor, Breeze was met by a tower of lockers that stretched further than she could see, and she immediately felt defeated. "How the hell am I supposed to find the right one in time?" She crouched down to the ground opposite the lockers and stared at them hopelessly. Suddenly, a locker in the corner began to glow, but Breeze wasn't paying attention.

"I need three minutes to get back to school, which gives me five minutes to find the medal. There's no way I can look through all these lockers in five minutes! They're so weird. Who builds lockers like this anyway? How can anyone reach the top ones? Why are they so narrow? Why's that one glowing? Why are they in–" Her rant was interrupted by her realisation. "Follow the glow," she whispered. She swiftly jumped to her feet and approached the locker. Breeze meticulously turned the dial to the combination: 22-2-04, but it didn't open. "Come on," she said as she tried again. After three failed attempts, Breeze was disrupted by two women walking out of the changing room. One was holding a baby.

"He's adorable! How old is he?"

"Five months," replied the baby's mother in an American accent. "He was born January 1st."

Breeze had an eureka moment. "She said January 1*st*, not 1*st* January. Benjamin Bailey was born in America... their dates are backwards!" She turned the dial to the combination: 2-22-04 and the locker quickly opened. The top of the locker was illuminating and as Breeze pushed it, a medal dropped into her hands. She let out a scream of excitement and quickly composed herself, tightly covering her mouth. "Four minutes, time to get out of here."

As Breeze walked to the staircase, she noticed two men walking towards her.

"Just down at the end of this corridor, I'll show you which locker needs to be removed," the manager explained.

Breeze smirked as their paths crossed and once she was sure that she was out of sight, she clicked her feet and soared back to school.

"Thirty seconds to spare," said Bella. "You cut it close!"

"Bell, that was harder than we planned. The date was in the American order. February 22nd. Not 22nd February."

"Oh course, he was born in the States. We didn't think of that. So, the month came before the day."

"Exactly."

"Why do they record the date like that anyway? It's so backwards."

"That's what I said."

"Did you get the medal?"

"Yeah, look."

"Wow. That's so sick! Put it in your bag somewhere safe. Good work, Breezy!"

"One down, two to go."

"Yep! That's the bell, let's go!"

"One second, I need to change into my school shoes."

"We've got P.E. now, Breeze. It don't matter. Come on."

The girls ran to their lesson and Chanel watched them from upstairs, through the common room window. "What are they doing?" she whispered.

"Why are you arriving to my lesson in trainers, Breeze?" said Mr Peters.

"Sorry, Sir, I just thought I'd save time by changing into them before the lesson."

"A logical explanation *if* this was a practical lesson. This period is a theory lesson and next period is your practical. But you know this already, Breeze, don't you? So, I'll ask again. *Why* are you wearing your trainers?"

"It's my fault, Sir," said Bella. "I got confused and thought we had our practical first, so I told Breeze to keep her trainers on."

"If it happens again, you'll have a detention, Breeze. Put your shoes on and take a seat."

"Yes, Sir."

Breeze quickly changed into her wallabees and threw her trainers into her bag.

"Right, settle down, Year 10," said Mr Peters. "In a moment, I am going to ask you to get into your teams and create a health and fitness plan for your client. Each group has a different client with specific health and dietary requirements. Using all we have learned this term, create a health and fitness plan for your client that's most suited to their needs. Each group will present their ideas to the class. You have twenty minutes. Off you go!"

The class left their seats and dispersed into groups. Chanel noticed that Breeze left her duffle bag under her chair and cunningly walked towards it. Subtly, as the class worked in their teams, creating mind-maps of their plans on A2 sugar paper, she switched Breeze's bag with Ade's and rushed to the door with the bag on her shoulder.

"And where are you going, Chanel?" said Mr Peters.

"Um – I need to go to the toilet," she replied, crossing her legs.

"You just had your break time. Stop avoiding doing work in my lessons."

Chanel did that frequently. She only chose P.E. as a GCSE option because Jayden was doing it.

"I'm not trying to get out of class, Sir, honestly," she insisted. "It's women's problems," she murmured. She knew this would work like a charm and it did.

"Hmm… You have five minutes," Mr Peter replied reluctantly.

Chanel locked herself in the female changing room and searched through the duffle bag. She pulled out Breeze's trainers and P.E. kit, throwing them to the ground.

"Useless!"

Followed by her deodorant.

"Nonsense."

Then her pencil case.

"Rubbish."

And finally, her textbooks.

"Argh! Waste of time! I know you're hiding something, Track Girl, and I will find out what it is."

She gathered Breeze's belongings, placed them back into the bag and hid it on top of the vent in the corner of the changing room.

"That was seven minutes," said Mr Peters as Chanel sauntered back into the lesson.

"Oh, was it? Sorry, Sir."

Each group presented their health and fitness plan whilst Mr Peters made notes on each presentation.

"It was very close," explained Mr Peters, "however, this group used scientific terminology fantastically. They also considered a range of exercises that their client could do, irrespective of his disability. So! The winners are… Team Bolt!"

Breeze's team jumped up and cheered as Mr Peters handed them a box of Celebrations.

"We did it, Breeze! We make a good team," said Jayden.

"I guess so," Breeze replied indifferently.

Chanel rolled her eyes at them. "Calm down, guys, it's only a box of chocolates!"

"Hater," said Jayden.

"Ok, ladies and gents, return to your seats and write the homework in your planners. Once you've got it down, you can head to the changing rooms and get ready for your practical."

As Breeze approached her desk, she could immediately tell that someone else's bag was under her chair. Her bag had a key chain of a heart on the zip, given to her by her grandmother.

"My bag," she uttered. "WHERE'S MY BAG?" she screamed.

"Breezy, what's wrong?" said Bella.

"This isn't my bag! My bag's gone!"

"Calm down, Breeze. I'm sure it's just been misplaced. Listen up, Year 10. Everyone check and make sure that you have the right bag," said Mr Peters. He checked the planner inside the bag under Breeze's chair. "Ade, this is yours," he said.

"So, who has mine?"

"Don't look at me. I ain't no teef," Ade replied.

Bella began to panic. "No, no, no! We have to find it, Breeze."

"My trainers... the medal," she whispered.

"Don't fret, girls, I'll email the reception and report it missing. If anyone hands it in, they'll bring it straight to you. Now off to the arena."

"But Sir, I need to go and look for it."

"Look for it? Where would you go? You had it last in this room. I'm sure someone's just picked it up by mistake. It will reappear. Let's go."

In the changing room, as Bella changed into her P.E. kit, Breeze retraced her steps.

"We'll find it, Breeze," said Bella.

"I had it in the lesson. I changed into my shoes and then we split into groups. No one left the lesson... did they?"

"I didn't see anyone leave the lesson, Breeze. It just doesn't make sense."

Breeze sat by the side of the track as her class completed a beep test. Chanel was on water duty. A duty she created herself because 'sweating was disgusting' and she refused to participate in any physical activities. Strangely, it was only Jayden and Ade who Chanel felt needed water. As she flirted with both boys, Breeze remembered overhearing Mr Peters' frustration with Chanel last period.

"YOU!" she yelled. She ran towards Chanel and rugby-tackled her to the ground. "Where did you put my bag!"

"Get off me! You're getting mud on my designer handbag! Someone help me! She's crazy!"

"You took my bag!" Breeze exclaimed as Bella pulled her away.

"Did I? I don't remember," she sneered.

"Enough!" Mr Peters shouted. "Breeze, go to the changing room and cool off!"

"But–"

"NOW!"

Breeze ran to the changing room and Bella followed her.

"Did you take her bag, Chanel?" Jayden asked.

"Maybe."

"That ain't cool, man. You're wrong for that," said Jayden, walking away.

"Gosh! Can't anyone take a joke anymore!"

Breeze paced up and down the changing room. "It was her, Bell! She took it!"

"Are you sure, Breeze?"

"Yes, she was the only person to leave the lesson. I overheard her saying something about women's problems to Sir." Bella began to march towards the door. "Where are you going, Bella?"

"I'm going to get your bag back and if she doesn't give it to me, I'm gonna ram her stupid Chanel handbag down her throat!" Breeze ran in front of Bella and slammed the door shut.

"No, she won't give it to us if we're forceful. Maybe we should tell her about the medals and saving the arena. Then she might help us."

"Breeze! Yeah, you've lost your damn mind."

Suddenly, Breeze noticed something glowing opposite her in the corner of the changing room. "Look – up there."

"It's glowing." Bella climbed on a bench and grabbed the bag. "Is this it, Breeze?"

"Yes! It is!" she replied, searching inside of it.

"Is everything in there? Your trainers? The medal?"

"Yeah. They're here. I put the medal in this little pocket here. Chanel would never have been able to find it."

"Oh my days! Yes!"

"Why would she do that to me, Bell? I thought we were cool now, she invited me to her party and everything."

"You never know how people really feel about you, Breeze. You need to be careful. Don't let that bag out of your sight again."

"I won't."

"It's almost lunchtime. Change into your trainers. You still got the timeline?"

"Yeah, it's in my pocket."

"Ok. So, Crystal Palace, historic wall. Behind the brick."

"Yeah. I remember."

The school bell rang. Bella held open the door to see if anyone was watching and as soon as she gave Breeze the all clear, off Breeze went. Crystal Palace Sports Centre was unusually busy as a primary school were on a trip visiting the grounds. Breeze checked the time and it had taken her ten minutes to run to the centre from her school.

"Ok, so that's twenty minutes, max, to find the medal and ten minutes to get back. Gosh, I sound like Bella."

Breeze walked into the sports centre and could not believe her eyes. The grounds were filled with tourists, athletes, children, teachers, and it was colossal! She noticed a man wearing a uniform and quickly approached him.

"Excuse me," she said, "do you work here?"

"Yes, love," replied an elderly man, "I've worked here for *fifty* years. It's the best job in the world! I've seen all sorts."

"Ahh, that's nice. Could you tell me–"

"Famous athletes, performances, riots, fights," he continued. "Did you know that there was once a robbery here? I mean, they only stole from the laundrette, but even still. They took off with over a hundred quid's worth of merchandise! The buggers. Anyway, I do love it here. I could've retired years ago but I can't think of anything else I would rather do. Crystal Palace has my heart!"

"Wow! That's amazing. You should be able to help me, then," replied Breeze impatiently.

"Of course, my dear, I know this place like the back of my hand."

"Great! I'm looking for the historic wall that honours famous athletes."

"Ah yes! That wall is remarkable. So much talent is recognised on that wall. It's a bit tricky to find, though. It's right at the end of the centre. If you ask me, I think they put it there on purpose so that people have to walk through the whole stadium and explore the place properly. Otherwise, people would just go straight to the wall and then bugger off!" he chuckled.

"That's what I'm trying to do," Breeze mumbled through a forced smile.

"Sorry, love, what did you say? My hearing's not great in my right ear."

"Oh, nothing. Could you tell me how to get to that wall, please?"

"Ok. So, you need to go straight down, past the restaurants and shops. Then, you've gotta turn right and walk past the stadium. Once there, you'll see an underground footpath, walk through that and then up the stairs."

"Thank yo—"

"Then, go around the back to a glass building, looks like a crystal. You need to go to the second floor in that building and bang! It's right there."

Breeze stood in a daze.

"It's ok, love, just remember: Restaurant and shops, do a right, underground, up the stairs, glass building and second floor. If you get stuck, there are signs to direct ya. You're looking for the Crystal Gallery."

Breeze typed his directions into her phone and noticed the time. "Ten minutes. I've got to use the boundless and beyond speed," she said to herself. "No, Breeze, it's too busy, people will see you disappear. Hmm… Ok, thank you for your help!" she said.

"I couldn't hear half of what you just said but you're very welcome, love!"

With a little help from her trainers, Breeze swiftly jogged to the wall and made it there in a few minutes. She could instantly see a brick glowing towards the bottom-left of the wall but there were too many visitors around the wall obstructing it.

"Come on, Breeze. Think, think, think." And before she knew it, Breeze had pretended to faint, right in front of the brick that she needed, conveniently.

"Danger! Danger!" cried the primary school children.

"Come on, kids, let's give her some space," said one of the teachers, ushering the children away. "We need a first aider, on the second floor. Quickly!"

Breeze pulled the glowing brick forward, her body facing the wall to hide her actions. She retrieved the medal and placed the brick back into the wall, moments before the first aider arrived.

"I'm fine now, thanks!" she said as she jumped up to her feet.

"What? No, I should check you over, just to make sure you're ok."

"No, no, I'm fine, really. I'm just a bit dehydrated. It's very warm today. A glass of water and I'll be fine."

"Ok, come with me and I'll get you some water."

"Oh, it's fine. I'll buy some on my way home. I only drink alkaline water."

"Me too! Come with me and I'll get you a bottle from our fridge."

"Ok. But do you mind if I just sit down here and wait for you to bring it to me, please? I feel a bit light-headed all of a sudden." Breeze held her head awkwardly to convince him.

"No problem. I'll be right back."

As soon as he left, Breeze went through the fire exit, clicked her heels and was back at the pond in nine minutes.

"Easy Breezy! You smashed it this time! We've still got five minutes till the bell goes."

"Thanks, Bella, but I'm shattered."

"I bet. You're doing so well. Did you get it?"

"Yeah, here," she said, handing Bella the medal and slumping on a log.

"Well done, Breeze. I got you a panini and a Ribena. Get that down ya," said Bella as she placed the medal in Breeze's bag.

"Thanks, Bella, I'm marvin'!" Breeze took as big of a bite that her mouth would allow and poured her juice down her throat.

"One more medal to go, Breeze and it's basically down the road, Mile End Stadium. Come on, let's start walking to Maths; the bell will go any minute now."

"I just thought that *I* should tell you, Mr Fraser because it's the right thing to do," said Chanel as the rest of the class lined up outside of the classroom. "I heard them planning it yesterday and Breeze was like 'Mr Fraser's so gullible, I'll just tell him that I need to go to the toilet towards the end of the lesson and he'll let me go!' I think that's really disrespectful, Sir. She's taking advantage because you're a safe teacher."

"So, she thinks she can trick me! I know every trick in the book. Thanks for letting me know, Chanel. You did the right thing."

"No problem, Sir," she replied with satisfaction.

"Come in, Year 10. Get your books out and start completing the equation on the board," said Mr Fraser. He watched Breeze suspiciously as she entered the room. "Afternoon, Breeze."

"Afternoon... Sir," Breeze replied, confused by his demeanour.

The day's events had taken its toll on Breeze and although she tried to resist, she was soon fast asleep. MC Hammer agreed to teach her the 'Hammer Dance' one last time but just he began, Breeze was awoken by three loud knocks on her table.

"Huh... 3.14 is pie," she said, wiping the dribble from the side of her mouth.

"What do you think this is? No sleeping in my classroom!" said Mr Fraser as he walked towards his desk.

"Sorry, Sir... wait, what's the time?" She looked down at her watch. "2:55, I've got to go." Breeze walked to Mr Fraser's desk and spoke as quietly as she could. Mr Fraser looked at Chanel and nodded. "Sir, I really need the toilet, could I leave a litt–"

"You're not going anywhere! Finish those equations or you'll be staying *after* the school bell."

"O-k," she replied, returning to her seat.

Mr Fraser gave Chanel a thumbs up.

"Right! Stand behind your chairs and wait for the bell," said Mr Fraser. As soon as it was three o'clock, Breeze charged for the door. "Wait there, Breeze. Come back here."

"I really need to go, Sir."

"And you can, once I've checked your work." He scanned her exercise book. "You haven't finished questions 4 and 5."

"Please, Sir, I'll do it for homework. I'll hand it in next lesson. Please."

"Hmm. I'm not a pushover, you know. I can be *cool*, but I ain't no *fool*."

"I know that, Sir. I always do my work and behave in your lessons. Today's just been a hard day for me. Please?"

"Ok, Breeze. Have it on my desk next lesson."

"Thanks, Sir. I will," she said, racing to the pond.

"These teenagers," said Mr Fraser, opening a pack of plantain chips and Jamaican Ginger Beer.

"You're still here! I thought you would've left already!" Bella exclaimed.

"Mr Fraser was being long for no reason, man. He wouldn't let me leave," Breeze replied, changing into her trainers.

"Ok, you've got eleven minutes. Good luck. I'll wait for you at the school reception."

"Ok, in a bit."

Breeze arrived at Mile End Stadium in under a minute. She was relieved to see how quiet the stadium was as she approached the help desk.

"Good afternoon, welcome to Mile End Stadium. My name's Helga and I'm here to help ya! Like what I did there? Helga... *help ya*. Rhymes with my name... It's Scandinavian, my dad's side of the family. Anyway, how can I help ya, hun?"

"Hi, Helga, could you show me where the tennis court is, please?"

"Court? As in one! Oh darlin', we have twenty-five tennis courts. They're just through those gates. I'll show ya."

Breeze followed Helga through the gates and stared in astonishment at the endless ocean of green that stretched far into the distance. "Damn," she gulped.

"Impressive, right?"

"Yeah, very impressive. Which court did Brian Bennett used to train in?"

"Brian Bennett! You've done your research. From what I can remember from our staff training, Brian only ever trained in one court. He used to say it was his lucky number, the number of his birthday. Now I can't remember if it was number two or number twenty-two. Hmm... let me think... I'm not sure, love. Sorry."

"Don't be sorry. You've been really helpful. Thank you, Helga."

Breeze looked at her watch and realised that she only had enough time to check one tennis court.

"Do I go for the day he was born, twenty-two *or* the month he was born in, two? Come on, Breeze, you don't have time for this."

Breeze's mind was in conflict, but it was suddenly calmed by a memory of Bella's voice: 'It says here he was twenty-two years old when he won the bronze medal.'

"Twenty-two!"

Breeze ran to court twenty-two and within seconds, saw a seat glowing in the stands on the opposite side of the tennis court. To her dismay, when she lifted seat number 38 in block 19, the medal had gone and all that was left was its imprint.

"No!" she said as the weight of her disappointment dragged her into the chair. She looked at the clock. "3:10," she sighed.

Meanwhile at Aspire Academy, the founders had already arrived and were waiting in the reception for the meeting to commence.

"Bella, may I have a word?" said Mrs Banjo, directing Bella into her office. "How did you girls get on today?"

"We've got two of the medals, Miss. Breeze is getting the third one as we speak."

"We've only got a few minutes before the meeting is due to start. Where are the two medals you collected?"

"In Breeze's bag."

"Right. And I'm guessing her bag is not here."

"Um, no… she's got it," said Bella contritely.

"Hmm, ok. I will do my best to stall the meeting, but I won't be able to hold them off for long."

"Ok, Miss. Breeze will be here soon."

As they left her office, Mrs Banjo looked at the clock in the main reception; it was 3:15. "We will be ready to begin in five minutes," she said.

"But we're all here and it's 3:15 already," said Dr Edwards, the Chief Executive of the Aspire Federation.

Mrs Banjo winked and her glasses began to glow, but Bella was the only person who could see it. She stared at the clock and the minute handle moved from the three to the two, marking ten minutes past three. "No, it's not," she replied. "Look."

Bella's mouth opened as she witnessed Mrs Banjo's manoeuvre.

"That's strange, I could have sworn it said quarter-past a moment ago. Regardless, we are all here so we may as well begin."

"Um, that's very true. You make an excellent point. However, we need to wait for the, um... for — the," Mrs Banjo noticed Stella, the school's chef, walking around the corner, pushing a trolley of refreshments.

"REFRESHMENTS!" Mrs Banjo shouted, startling the founders. "Sorry to yell. The refreshments," she repeated. Her left arm was behind the wall, hidden from the guests as she directed Stella to reverse like lollipop lady. Stella pulled back the trolley and reversed around the corner. "The refreshments will be here in five minutes," said Mrs Banjo, overenunciating so that Stella could hear her.

"Well, I hope they're worth the wait," said Dr Edwards.

"They will be," Mrs Banjo replied, walking into her office with a sense of triumph. Bella's eyes followed Mrs Banjo as she walked. "Close your mouth, dear; flies will get in," said Mrs Banjo, tapping Bella's shouldeBack at the stadium, Breeze had worked up a sweat, searching in between the seats, hoping to find the medal. The laughter of a toddler caught her attention and as Breeze looked up, she saw a little girl holding a glowing piece of silver.

"That's it." Breeze ran towards the child and was just about to grab the medal when her father called out, "Immy, Imogen! Come back here."

Breeze smiled and waved at Imogen's father. "She's ok. She just wants to play with these tennis balls!" Breeze cried as Imogen's father nodded, signalling his consent. Breeze remembered learning how to juggle in primary school and began to toss the tennis balls in the air, captivating Imogen's attention. "Ok, Immy. I'm gonna need you to give me that medal," said Breeze as she continued to juggle.

"NO!" Imogen retorted.

"What?" said Breeze in shock, cautious that Imogen's father was watching her. She smiled at him and knelt down to hand Imogen a ball. Imogen took the ball, threw it in Breeze's face and started laughing.

"Look, I don't have time for this," said Breeze, snatching the medal from Imogen's hands. Imogen's lip began to quiver, and she screamed as tears left her eyes.

"No, no, no. Please. Don't cry. You don't want this boring piece of metal. Here, have this ball."

Imogen threw the ball at Breeze again and screamed even louder as her father jogged towards them.

"Ok, ok, look. Um," said Breeze, searching through her pockets. "Here you go, a pound coin." And as if by magic, Imogen stopped crying.

"Is she ok?" said her father.

"Yeah. She got a bit upset when she couldn't juggle the tennis balls, but I gave her a coin I had in my pocket and she settled."

"Oh, you shouldn't have, let me give you your money back."

"Oh, it's fine, honestly. I've got to go now anyway. Take care!"

"Ok. Bye, say bu-bye, Imogen."

Breeze waved as she walked towards the exit. She looked around and when no one was watching, she clicked her heels and shot off.

"Right, the refreshments are here now. What else are we waiting for? It's twenty-past three!" said Dr Edwards.

"No, it's not, it's just turned three-fifteen. Look," replied Mrs Banjo, pointing at the clock.

"Well your clock is incorrect. *Look*," Dr Edwards retorted, holding up his phone.

Mrs Banjo realised her time was up. "Oh yes, you're right. My sincere apologies. If you would like to follow me to our conference room."

"Just a few more minutes, Miss," Bella whispered.

"It's ok, dear. You did your best," she replied dejectedly.

Minutes later, Breeze ran into the reception. "I got it! I put all the medals on Mrs Banjo's desk! Where is she? Where are the founders?"

"It's too late, Breeze. They just went into the meeting."

"What? No!"

"I know. We tried, Breezy. Wait, how did you — I didn't see you come into school."

"I came in through the back entrance. I didn't want the founders to see me running in."

"Ah, I see. You were so close, Breeze."

"All that work for nothing."

Breeze's back was against the wall as she slid to the ground. She buried her head in between her knees and Bella placed her arm around her shoulders.

"No," Breeze whispered.

"No what?"

"We have to try."

Breeze jumped up and marched towards the conference room.

"Wait for me!" said Bella, scuttling behind her.

"I think we're all in agreement that Mrs Banjo has done an outstanding job, but it is now time to evolve. Bring back traditional subjects such as Latin. Encourage students to pick up an instrument rather than a javelin or discus. Broaden their horizons," Dr Edwards declared. "So, without any *further* delay, if you can each read the agreements in front of you and sign them once you have done so."

"MRS BANJO!" Breeze yelled, knocking vigorously on the window.

"Good heavens! What's going on?" said Dr Edwards.

Mrs Banjo rose to her feet hastily and Breeze gave her a thumbs up.

"WAIT!" said Mrs Banjo. "I'm sorry, could I ask you to put your pens down for *one* moment, please?"

"My goodness! What is the delay now?" said Dr Edwards.

"I will be back in *two* minutes. This is such a final and impactful decision; we should consider all factors before going ahead. Two minutes, that's all I ask for... please?"

"Fine," Dr Edwards replied.

Mrs Banjo rushed through the door. "Where are they, Breeze?" she said.

"On your desk, Miss."

Mrs Banjo ran to her office, leaving Breeze and Bella standing unnervingly at the door and the bemused founders staring at them.

"Hi," they said concurrently.

"Breeze! Is that you? It is! Oh, Breeze!" said Eliza, one of the founders, rising to her feet and walking towards the door. "You probably don't recognise me without my shades and gym gear on. You saved my cat! Baby Breeze."

"Baby Breeze," Bella repeated, holding back her laughter as Breeze elbowed her.

"Oh yeah. Hi again," said Breeze.

"Good to see you. I didn't know you were an Aspire student."

"Yeah. I love this school. It's where I learned how to run. I train in that arena twice a week; I'm gutted that it's closing down." The expression of joy on Eliza face was quickly replaced with guilt.

As Mrs Banjo entered her office, she was stunned to see the three medals on her desk. "Incredible," she whispered, "they actually did it."

She picked them up and carefully placed them in the Aspire Coat of Arms adjacent to her office. Instantly, the Coat of Arms began to glow and emitted a light that shone through the entire reception. Mrs Banjo was overcome with happiness and tears ran down her face profusely. She gathered herself and returned to the conference room to find Breeze and Bella entertaining the founders with Stevie Wonder's 'Happy Birthday'. Breeze played a beat using the table and her hands, whilst Bella sang, and the founders clapped along.

"It was my birthday yesterday, so Breeze and Bella performed a song for me. So *adorable*. Are you aware that Breeze saved my baby? She's a very talented runner," said Eliza as she returned to her seat.

"Saved your baby?" Mrs Banjo replied in confusion.

"Long story, Miss," said Bella.

"Anyway, thank you for your patience. Breeze, Bella, could you wait in the reception, please?"

"Ok, Miss. Bye, everyone," said Bella.

"Bye," said Breeze.

"They are lovely girls," said Eliza.

"Yes, they are, and they have done something remarkable. Something unbelievable."

"Well? Spit it out," said Dr Edwards.

"They have found the stolen medals from the Aspire Coat of Arms."

"Impossible!" Dr Edwards objected.

"That's what I thought, but I assure you, they have found them and returned them. Please follow me."

Mrs Banjo escorted the founders to the reception and stood before the Coat of Arms.

Dr Edwards inspected the medals and was short of words. "Unbelievable! – How? – When?"

"Dr Edwards, founders. I present to you the Aspire Coat of Arms. This medal belonged to Benjamin Bailey. Aspire class of 1920 and Olympic Silver Medallist for Swimming, in 1924. This medal belonged to Bianca Baker. Aspire class of 1925 and Olympic Gold Medallist for the 400 metre hurdles in 1932. This medal was awarded to Brian Bennett. Aspire class of 1954 and Bronze Medallist for wheelchair tennis in the *first ever* Paralympics in 1960. And finally, this medal belongs to me, Beverley Banjo. Aspire class of 1993 and Olympic Silver Medallist for the triple jump in 1996. This school has nurtured and educated exceptional athletes. Sport is in Aspire's DNA. It teaches our students how to be resilient individuals, team players, and hardworking students, prepared to take the world by storm! It's in our history. Please don't take that away from these kids."

The founders looked at each other sombrely. "I can't – I won't take away the sporting specialism from this school. It's too precious," said Eliza, tearing her agreement.

"Hear, hear," said another founder, also ripping his agreement. "Sport is at the heart of this institution."

"I... I... *agree*," said Dr Edwards. "These medals are worth a great deal of money and their value will increase with time. However, the stories and achievements behind them are both inspiring and sacred, worth more than any amount of money. In light of their return, I am willing provide additional funding to sustain the arena for another five years. However, we must build a secure cabinet of some sort to ensure they are not taken again."

"I agree and I will match your five years of funding," said Eliza.

The founders signed an agreement to fund the arena and sporting initiatives at Aspire Academy, Poplar for another twenty years with a possible extension if the school continued to perform successfully. Breeze and Bella had been listening from the top of the staircase and once the founders left, they raced down the stairs, screaming with excitement and squeezed Mrs Banjo.

"You did it, girls. You saved our school. You saved our arena," said Mrs Banjo tearfully.

"No, Miss. *We* did it," said Breeze.

15

On the Telly

The following Monday, an urgent, whole school assembly was called at the end of the day.

"Good afternoon, ladies and gents. I'm sure you have heard the news, but I am pleased to confirm that our academy will remain a sports specialist institution and the planned arena closure will no longer go ahead. I am also pleased to announce that I am not stepping down as your Principal and I'm honoured to continue to lead you as a school. Honestly, this is fantastic news and we are very fortunate to be in this position. I would like to thank Breeze and Bella in Year 10 for their outstanding effort to find the stolen medals. You have made history, girls, and you should be extremely proud of yourselves. Please join me in giving them a round of applause."

Bella slowly stood up, expecting Breeze to join her. Breeze didn't.

"Why are you standing, Bell?"

"I don't know. Ain't that what we're supposed to do? They're all clapping for us."

"Nah, I'm good. Please sit down now, Bell."

"Fine."

But it was too late. Just as Bella began to take her seat, Mrs Banjo noticed them. "That's right, Bella," said Mrs Banjo. "Breeze don't be shy. Please stand."

"Ah, man. See what you did, Bella!" Breeze groaned, reluctantly rising from her chair.

"Thank you, ladies. You may be seated. What a brilliant way to begin our penultimate week of the school year as we prepare for Sports Day on Wednesday. Before I conclude, I would like to play a short video clip from last Friday's BBC news report."

Mrs Banjo switched off the lights and the report began to play on the projector. "The medals were stolen over fifty years ago and despite the efforts of the authorities, they were not retrieved," said the reporter. "However, two 15-year-old students: Breeze Bassey and Bella Balivo of Tower Hamlets, East London, managed to trace these medals and return them to their school. I'm joined today by both girls and Beverley Banjo, Principal of Aspire Academy, Poplar, here in our studio. Congratulations, girls! You must be so proud of yourselves; you're heroes!"

"Thank, you. Yeah, we're proud, but mainly we're just so happy that our school arena won't be closing down," said Bella.

"That's right. I understand that finding the medals has provided Aspire with the funding required to keep the arena open," the reporter replied. "Why does that mean so much to you, Breeze?"

"Um, because sport is what makes our school so special. So many of us train in that arena and it's where the whole school comes together for events. Like, we've got Sport's Day next week and things like that. My school life wouldn't be the same without it," said Breeze.

"Remarkable. Beverley, one could say that finding these medals was nothing short of a miracle!"

"Yes, they did a fantastic job. I don't know how they did it, whist being exemplary students and dedicated athletes. We are all very grateful to them. I'm one proud principal."

As Mrs Banjo switched off the projector, the assembly hall erupted with celebrations. The noise transcended the school walls and for once, Mrs Banjo didn't mind it.

"Look at your big head on the telly!" Bella chortled.

"I don't know why you're laughing, mate. My head ain't no bigger than yours, darlin'! I can't believe that we were actually on the telly, though. Mama I made it!"

"Trust! My mum recorded it and everything!"

"Same. My mum did the most! She even called my grandma in Nigeria and I had to speak to her for ages while she spoke blessings over my life!"

"Swear! That's sweet, though. I'm so proud of you, Breeze. Even though you were so tired and faced some challenges along the way, you figured it out and just did it. You were amazing."

"Thank you, Bell, but I couldn't have done it without your help, man. The timekeeping, organisation, and your *very* detailed plan. We bossed it!"

As Breeze and Bella did the B Squared handshake, they were surrounded by students congratulating them.

"Nice one, girls. I don't know how I would've been able to keep training if we lost the arena. Thank you," said Jayden. He was followed by numerous students and members of staff praising the girls' achievement.

Finally, Chanel wanted to express her appreciation. "That was cool, girls. I rate you for that, seriously. Oh, and Breeze — sorry about the whole bag thingy."

"Thanks, Chanel and it's all good," Breeze replied.

"*Bag thingy!* Wow. So cheeky," said Bella as she watched Chanel walk away.

"That's the best apology you can expect from Chanel, Bella."

"Ladies and gentlemen, may I have your attention, please?" said Mrs Banjo to a frenzied audience. "Settle down, now... Take your seats... Guys... BE QUIET!" Instantly, the hall was silent. "Just one final thing from me, then you may be dismissed... WHO'S READY FOR SPORTS DAY?"

The students began to chant "A-A-P! A-A-P! A-A-P!" at the top of their voices. Filled with happiness, Mrs Banjo winked at Breeze and Bella, causing her glasses to glow.

Bella's jaw dropped as remembered the day of the founder's meeting. "Oh yeah! Glasses!" she said. "Boy, I've got something to tell you about Mrs B, Breeze!"

"What? What now? ... Here we go."

– 16 –

Sports Day

The annual Federation Sports Day had always been an electrifying event at Aspire Academy, the most anticipated day of the year. All students from the schools in Homerton, Bow, Leyton, and Beckon, gathered at the Poplar academy's arena for the day. This year, however, was the most extravagant Sports Day yet. The students and staff of Poplar made a special effort this year: vibrant banners adorned the stadium, groups of dancers performed to the rhythms of the steel pan band and the canteen staff provided a barbecue with enough food to feed a small village! The recent solving of the infamous 'stolen medal case' and the media coverage that accompanied it, brought nationwide attention to this Sports Day, with reporters from local and national news outlets in attendance. Oga D and Uncle D collaborated to make takeaway goodie bags for all competitors. The day was even sponsored by KA drinks, who provided everyone with a free can! Famous Aspire alumni came down to support, and the event was officially opened with a live performance by Brit Award winning duo, Trillz and Skillz.

The field events took place first and it was Bella's turn to compete.

"Go on, Bella! You got this!" cheered Breeze from the stands.

Bella stumbled as she threw her javelin into the air. She watched in disappointment as it plummeted towards the grass. Sixty-six point three metres was the leading score achieved by Rene, a student from Aspire Academy, Bow, and although this was lower than Bella's personal best, she knew that she had not given her greatest performance. As Mr Peters measured her distance, Bella had already prepared herself for the worst.

"And the final distance is..." he announced, pausing to create tension. "Sixty..." he deliberately delayed, "... seven point one metres!"

Bella calculated and realised that her score was the furthest distance. "Oh my gosh! No way! I won! I–"

"YOU WON!" Breeze bellowed, pouncing on her best friend.

"I WON!" Bella replied as they rolled on the ground.

Their celebrations were paused by Breeze's observation. "Everyone's staring at us, Bell," said Breeze.

"Who cares!" they cried simultaneously, continuing their merrymaking.

"That was so close, Breeze. I thought I wouldn't do it."

"I knew you would, Bell. Come on! My bestie and that!" Breeze began to dance, "Go best friend! That's my best friend!"

"Thanks, Breezy! Damn, I need to sit down," said Bella, returning to the stands. She slouched in her seat and said, "Ah, now I can chill! Just sit back and enjoy the show."

"Lucky you," Breeze replied nervously.

"Don't stress, Breeze. You'll be ok."

"Well, it's long jump now and then it's the racing events so I've still got some time."

Breeze and Bella watched the participants compete. Each competitor was supported by their school with posters, whistles, chants, and cheers. Traditionally, the students from the host school were last to compete in each event and it was now Jayden's turn.

"Look, Jayden's up next," said Breeze.

"Mm-hmm... And why did your eyes light up when you said that? Huh?"

"No, they didn't."

"Yeah they did."

"No – they didn't."

"Aww."

"*Stop,* Bella."

"Ok, I'll stop... for now."

Jayden looked over at Breeze as he waited to run. Breeze mouthed the words 'good luck' and gave him a smile of encouragement. He nodded back at her and then his focus swiftly shifted to the sandpit. He started to clap rhythmically above his head, beckoning the crowd to join in. The crowd's claps were a wave of support that flowed through the stadium and mirrored his heartbeat. Impulsively, he was propelled by his feet, increasing in speed as he approached the take-off point. He leaped into the air, his legs rotating as if he was riding a bicycle. As he started to incline, he stretched out his legs as far he could, and his heels hit the sand.

Jayden turned to the commentator awaiting his result. "10.58 metres". Once he realised that he had finished in second place, Jayden leaped up and starting rapping 'U Can't Touch This' by MC Hammer and did the 'Shuffle Dance' towards the stands.

Chanel was unimpressed. "What is he doing? That's so cringey," she said.

"Allow it, Jayden," said Ade.

"You lot ain't ready for them tunes there, innit, Breeze."

"Come on! Hammer's a G!" she replied.

"That's embarrassing," Chanel sneered.

"Whatever, Chanel. Nobody cares about what you think," said Jayden.

Chanel was surprised by Jayden's response. She frowned at him as he walked towards Breeze. He sat down beside Breeze and the noise of the crowd was drowned out by her words, "Well done, J."

"Thank you, Breeze."

"I thought that the *National Champ* for long jump can't listen to MC Hammer?"

"Who said that foolishness?"

Breeze tilted her head and replied, "Err, *you*."

"I know, I know. But you showed me different, B. There's no point trying to fit in with the crowd if it means you lose yourself. I deeped that when you said it. I get it. You were right, B."

"I'm glad you see what I was saying. You don't need to act no different, J – you're cool just how you are."

"Was that a compliment?"

"Nope," Breeze sharply replied.

"I swear it was, Bella?"

"It defo was."

"Oh, you two are annoying," said Breeze.

"I'm just messing with you," said Jayden. His self-assured demeanour swiftly subsided and he was filled with nerves. "So, um, Breeze, I… I–"

"You all right, J?" she said.

"Yeah, I'm good. I was just thinking, well not just thinking. I've *been* thinking… Would you like to go for dinner sometime, maybe Nando's, get a little chicken and that?"

"Yeah, that would be nice. I'd like that."

"Yeah?"

"Yeah."

"All right, cool. I'll text ya… or call or… yeah."

"Ok then."

Bella stared and them as they stared and each other. Jayden felt Bella's glare and composed himself.

"Anyway, I should go and check on the man dem. Good luck, Breeze. I'll be watching from the side of the track. Go and body the ting! In a bit, girls."

"Thank you, J. See ya."

"Later, Jayden," said Bella.

Breeze watched Jayden as he walked away until her eyes met Bella's, peering at her intensely.

"Aww," Bella sighed.

"Shut up, man."

"You two are so cute."

"Ain't nothing cute about me."

"So sweet," Bella continued.

"Your mum's sweet," Breeze scoffed.

"Your mum's sweeter. Your mum's so sweet that they call her brown sugar!"

"Oh yeah? Well your mum's so sweet that — that — yeah, you won that one, Bell."

The girl's amusement was disrupted by an announcement through the tannoy speaker. "Would the representatives for the female 100-metre sprint from each school, please make their way to the starting line. I repeat, women's 100-metre sprint to the starting line. Thank you."

"That's you, Breezy."

"Bell... I'm scared."

"Breeze, come on. We've been training for this day. You're ready for this."

"I don't know, Bell. Tanya would have beaten me at the heats if it wasn't for my trainers. They're in my bag... a part of me wants to change into them."

"Seriously? Why are you so worried about Tanya? Focus on yourself! Breeze, remember how you felt after you won that race. Do you really want to win by cheating... *again*?"

"No, I don't want that. It's just... everyone expects me to win. What will they say if I lose after my last victory?"

"Since when did you start doing things based on what other people would think of you? Look at how you helped Jayden be true to himself, you need to take your own advice. You know what's right, Breeze. Don't lose that for nobody."

"You're right, Bell."

"I always am," Bella jested. "If you're gonna win this thing, Breeze, do it the right way: fair and square."

"That's right. And if I don't win, I did my best."

"Exactly! Now you're talking. If you did you best..."

"Big up my chest."

"Come on! Say it again!" said Bella, standing in exhilaration.

"If I did my best, big up my chest!" Breeze repeated.

"That's it. Now hurry up, they're waiting for you."

Breeze knelt at the starting line and looked over at Tanya who was beside her. "Good luck, Tanya."

"Thanks, Breeze. You too."

Breeze looked towards the finish line whilst she waited for the shot of the starting pistol. The sounds of the arena became blurred as she began to think about Bella's pep talk. "Do your best, big up your chest," she murmured. Her eyes caught the glance of the caretaker, seated in the stands. He gave her a thumbs up and she smiled back at him. For the first time, she could see his name clearly written on his cap and read it out:

"Lance… Lance! Is that you?" she whispered to herself. His face lit up as she realised who he was, and he nodded. Breeze was elated and the realisation that Lance had always been there, so close by for all these years was the ultimate boost of encouragement that she needed.

Mr Peters raised his pistol and called out, "On your marks." Breeze positioned herself and looked down at her hands. "Get set." She raised her back and looked up ahead at her goal. "GO!"

Breeze's felt a rush of energy shoot through her body as Mr Peters pulled the trigger. Her attention was fixed on her lane and she was unaware that Tanya was by her side. She soon gained momentum and her speed accelerated rapidly.

"Come on, Breezy!" yelled Bella from the stands.

Before long, Breeze was considerably ahead of her opponents. Breeze crossed the finish line in 14.92 seconds, winning the race and exceeding her personal best.

"Yes! Come on, Breezy!" Bella screamed, running to meet Breeze at the finished line. "Go best friend! That's my best friend!"

Breeze lay on the track, overwhelmed by her achievement.

"That's how you do it, B!" said Jayden as he helped her stand up.

"Thank – you – guys. Thanks – so – much! I – can't – believe – it," Breeze panted. Suddenly, Breeze remembered seeing her old friend. "Lance!" Her eyes began to search through the crowds when she saw Lance, standing across the stadium. She winked at him first this time and he winked back before leaving the arena.

"Congratulations, Breeze. You were sick!" said Tanya. "Aspire Poplar are killing it today, boy!"

"Thanks, Tanya! Congrats on coming second."

"Thanks. I beat my PB as well so I'm proper happy."

"That's sick," said Breeze.

"I'm proud of you, girl," said Bella. "See, you didn't need the trainers to win; it was in you all along."

"Thanks, Bell. Thanks for helping me do the right thing. Listen, I need to change into my tracksuit and trainers, get me some jerk chicken and chill."

"Amen to that! Let's go," said Bella.

"Well done, Breeze!" said Ade.

"Yeah, congratulations!" said Chanel.

"Thanks, guys," Breeze replied as she walked with Bella to the stands.

"Why you always following me, Ade?" said Chanel.

"Seriously! You're following *me*, Chan! You're a joker."

"You wish."

"No Chan, I know. And I know you like me, but you don't want to admit it because you think that as the most popular girl in the school, you should be with the most popular guy, an athlete. You need to hurry up and get over that for real, cause I'm *here,* innit. But I ain't gonna be here forever. All this chocolate should be illegal! You know like that!" said Ade.

"Oh please. Get over yourself."

"Yeah, yeah. When you're ready, Chan. See you later," said Ade. Chanel smirked as she watched Ade walk away.

"I know you're watching me!" he yelled, and Chanel briskly turned to walk in the opposite direction.

"Breeze! Bella! Gwan, my girls! Big up yourself," said Uncle D.

"Well done! Well done, my girls!" said Oga D. "It's nice to see you two together again."

"Thank you," Breeze chuckled.

"Yeah thanks," said Bella, winking at Oga D.

"We're starving. What have you got for us today?" said Bella.

"Oh, don't worry!" said Oga D. "You trust me, now! You know we will look after you!"

"Yes! Yes! Nah worry 'bout it. Everything you need is in ya goodie bag."

"Thank you so much!" said Bella, clasping her bag.

"Thanks, guys," said Breeze.

"You're welcome," Oga D replied. He began to laugh to himself and suddenly roared at Breeze. Breeze jumped back and almost dropped her food.

"Ok, bye!" said Bella, swiftly pulling Breeze away.

"What was that about, Bell? Why's he just roaring in my face like that?"

Bella looked back at Oga D and giggled. "I ain't got a clue, Breeze."

B Squared

The awards ceremony was typically the less exciting part of Sports Day. Breeze would always complain about how long it was, and every year, Bella would ask a senior member of staff if they could go home early and collect their medals the next day, to which she always received a firm 'No'. However, this year, former AAP student and British Olympic athlete for the 400-metres race, Kerri Brayton, was handing out the medals and B Squared were ecstatic.

"Bell."

"Yes."

"Did I just meet Kerri Brayton?"

"Yep."

"Did she just place a medal around my neck?"

"Yep."

"Did I really shake her hand?"

"Yep."

"I thought so. I'm not washing these hands again."

"Yes, you are, that's nasty," said Bella.

"Yeah, that's dirts. I will be washing them… at some point, but damn!"

"I know, Breeze. This has been the best Sports Day, man! For real."

"Defo."

"Hold my food for a sec, Breeze; I need to put my hair up. It's so hot!"

"Yeah, it's baking today."

Bella tied her hair up in a ponytail and wrapped it into a bun.

"Thanks, Breeze," said Bella, seizing her container.

"I like your hair up like that, Bell – suits ya. You should wear it up more often."

"Thanks, you think so? My ears stick out a bit but, oh well."

"Oh please. No, they don't."

"Yes, they do."

Suddenly, Bella clutched her ears in discomfort.

"What's all that noise?" she said.

"What noise?" said Breeze.

Bella could hear a combination of several conversations in the arena blaring in her ears.

"Bell, are you ok?"

"Yeah, I think so. It's stopped now. That was strange."

Breeze stared at Bella with a look of incredulity.

"What? Why are you looking at me like that?" said Bella. "You're looking at my ears? See, I told you. I'll just take this bun out."

"No! Not your ears. Your *earrings*."

"Yeah. My birthday earrings. What about them? Why are you being weird, Breezy?"

"They're glowing. Your earrings, Bell… they're glowing."

"No, they're not, Breeze. It's probably just the crystals in the sunlight."

"Bell, I swear," said Breeze. She tapped the shoulders of the people sitting in front of them and said, "Excuse me, do see her earrings glowing?" Both students looked at Breeze impassively and turned around. Breeze took out her phone, opened the camera app and held it up in Bella's face.

"Oh my days! Breeze, they're glowing!"

"That's what I've been saying!"

"Do you hear that?" said Bella. She could hear a conversation coming from a building behind the stadium.

"What can you hear, Bell? … Bell?"

"Watch… they're talking about a watch."

"Who's talking?"

"I don't know… he said… he said it's… it's glowing."

"What?"

"His watch is glowing. They're here. They're Aspire students."

"Ok. This is mad. Where are they?"

"I don't know, but they said they're in a room."

Breeze noticed a light in the distance. "Bell, look," she said, pointing towards it.

"No way. Why is that building glowing, Breeze?"

"I don't know, Bell."

"Maybe that's where the boys are."

"Boys?"

"Yeah, it's two boys I can hear talking."

"Remember what the card said, Bell: 'follow the glow'."

"Let's go check it out."

Breeze and Bella discreetly left the stands and walked to the end of the stadium in the direction of the light. They arrived at a closed door, but the surrounding area was desolate.

"Open the door, Breeze."

"Why me? You open it."

"This is creepy, I think we should go back."

"No, we're here now. Ok, I'll open it." Breeze placed her hand on the doorknob and cautiously began to turn it. "Three... two... two and a half... two and three-quarters... one... nought point five..."

"Breeze!"

"Ok, ok. Three... two..."

Just as Breeze was about to pull the door, a student pushed it open from the other side, causing Breeze and Bella to scream uncontrollably.

"I'm sorry! I didn't mean to scare ya. I'm Bashir and that's Bailey."

Breeze and Bella quickly calmed and entered the room.

"Hi, I'm Bella."

"Hey, I'm Breeze. What is this place?"

"I don't know. This is *your* school's arena. We saw it glowing and thought we'd check it out," said Bashir.

"Yeah, we saw that too... I've never noticed this place before," Breeze replied.

"What Aspire Academy are you two from?" asked Bella.

"Bow," they both replied.

"Wait a minute, all our names begin with B," said Bailey.

"Yeah... I don't think that's a coincidence," said Bella.

"Wait... when are your birthdays?" Breeze asked.

"We've got the same birthday," said Bashir.

"Course you do. Don't say it's—"

"2nd February," said Breeze and Bashir.

"Yeah, because we're double the trouble," Bailey chuckled. "How did you know?"

"Me and Bella were born on 2nd February too."

"Yeah, because the best things come in twos," said Bella.

"2002?" asked Bailey.

"Yep."

"Same year as us. This is crazy," said Bashir.

"Tell me about it," said Breeze. "Bailey, your watch is glowing."

"Wow. Someone else who can actually see it, Bashir. Yeah, I got it for my birthday. Your trainers are glowing too... and Bella's earrings."

"Wait a minute," said Breeze, "You can see them glowing, Bailey?"

"Well it's hard to miss," said Bashir.

Breeze and Bella looked at each other, their mouths wide open.

"Your cap, Bashir. It's glowing too," said Bella.

"Rah, you can see it. I thought only Bailey could see it. My dad bought it as one of my b-day gifts. Can you see it glow too, Breeze?"

"Yeah... Yeah I can."

Silence filled the room as they tried to make sense of what was happening. Unexpectedly, the doorknob turned.

"Who's that?" Breeze whispered.

As the door creaked, they flocked together. The door swayed open, but the sunlight from outside made them unable to decipher who was standing by it.

"Unbelievable... It all makes sense now," said Mrs Banjo, closing the door behind her. "Look at you all... look at how you all glow."

"Mrs B?" said Bella. "Do you know what's going on?"

"I think I have an idea. What's your gift, Breeze?"

"Gift?" she replied.

"Yeah, your power. Based on your trainer's glow, I'm guessing it's something to do with your feet... It's ok, Breeze, you can trust me."

"Um. Yeah. I can run really fast."

"But you run fast anyway," said Mrs Banjo.

"No, I mean *really* fast. Like super-fast. With my trainers I can run so fast that no one can see me."

"Amazing. And you, Bella. What's your gift?"

"I just discovered it today, but I think it's my hearing, Miss. I can hear things that are really far away."

"Brilliant! You will probably be able to fine-tune your hearing to specific sounds and locations as you get used to it. And you, young man?"

"Oh me? I can stop time," said Bailey.

"Swear down! That's sick!" said Bella.

"*Sick*, indeed," said Mrs Banjo. "And yourself? I see your cap is glowing."

"Yeah. I'm a walking encyclopaedia with this cap. I can find out and solve pretty much anything in seconds," Bashir replied.

"Fantastic. That will be so useful to your team," said Mrs Banjo.

"Team?" said Breeze.

"Yes. Team, you'll see."

"And what about you, Miss?" said Bella.

"Me?"

"Yes, you. I saw you the other day with the clock – I saw your glasses glowing."

"Fine. You've caught me red-handed. I can move anything with my eyes."

"Like Matilda!" said Bella.

"Yes, you could say that. But those days are behind me, I've been out of the game for a long time now. *You* all must be the next generation."

"Miss, what do you mean? I'm baffled!" said Breeze.

Mrs Banjo began to laugh spontaneously. "Incredible! You guys don't know what you're in for, but you have an exciting adventure ahead of you! Good luck!" she chuckled as she left the room.

"Wait! Miss! … Don't leave," said Bailey.

"Sports Day's over, guys. Everyone's leaving and I need to lock up," said Lance.

"Lance!" yelled Breeze as she ran and bear hugged him.

"It's good to see you, Breeze."

"You too! I can't believe you've worked here for all these years and I didn't recognise you!"

"A lot has changed since I last saw you… I *live* close by."

"Live?" tears began to fill Breeze's eyes.

"Yes, live. Now, now, Breeze. No tears. We'll catch up at another time, but I need to lock up soon."

"Ok, we'll be out in five minutes."

"No problem, I'll give you ten. Look, Breeze, you dropped your keys," said Lance, walking towards the door. Lance watched as Breeze picked them up. He gave her a wink and said, "Hold it tight," before closing the door behind him.

"I will, Lance. I will."

"Breeze, look," said Bella.

"What?"

"Your keyring. The penny… it's glowing."

"Yeah, I see it too," said Bailey. "Who is that guy?"

"Breeze? Say something."

"Um… who is he… that's Lance. But…"

"But what?"

For the first time, as she looked at her keyring, Breeze believed in magic. Her mind displayed a trailer of her encounters with Lance: from the day he gave her that 'magic' penny and the luck she felt it brought her ever since, to the way he would support B Squared's training and how he was always conveniently around to assist them when they had a premises issue at school. Not to mention the birthday card she found in her shoebox from a mystery 'faithful friend' who had 'always been close by'. As she watched the penny glow for the very first time, she realised that Lance was more special than she could have ever imagined.

"Come on, Breezy," Bella prompted. "That's Lance, *but*…"

"But… but *who* is Lance?"

Without realising, the four students stood in a square, light emitting from the ground in between them. They were in awe, overwhelmed by their newfound connection. In that moment they knew that their summer was about to be like none other.

Breeze was astounded. Examining her new alliances, she began to hypothesise once again. Her theory was in its initial stages; however, she was able to make one conclusion from her findings. "Bella...?" she said.

"Yeah..."

"I... I think B Squared's just expanded."